Dr. Shivers' Carnival

Look for these SpineChillers™ Mysteries

Dr. Shivers' Carnival

Fred E. Katz

Thomas Nelson, Inc.
Nashville

Published in Nashville, Tennessee, by Tommy Nelson™, a division of Thomas Nelson, Inc. SpineChillers™ Mysteries is a trademark of Thomas Nelson, Inc.

Scripture quoted from the *International Children's Bible, New Century Version,* copyright © 1983, 1986, 1988 by Word Publishing, Dallas, Texas. Used by permission.

Storyline: Tim Ayers

ISBN 0–8499–4056–7

Printed in the United States of America.

A blood-chilling scream woke me up. I jumped from the bed in my uncle's guest room and slid across the hardwood floor to the window.

I couldn't believe what I saw. In the field next to my uncle's Hollywood house was a carnival! It wasn't there when I arrived yesterday from the airport. It wasn't there last night when I went to bed. Where had it and the scream come from?

I grabbed my robe and ran out of the room and down the long hallway to the stairs. As I raced down the stairs and into the family room, I heard my uncle talking in the kitchen. He was hanging up the telephone when I walked through the kitchen doorway.

"Uncle Rex, where did the carnival come from?" I asked.

"That's exactly why I was on the phone. The local police said that the carnival owners rented the field to put up their carnival. It looks like it'll be there for a few days," he told me.

"So, what do we do now, Uncle Rex?" I was hoping he'd say that I could go over and see the carnival.

Uncle Rex pretended like he was thinking really hard. "Now, let me see here, Kyle. Maybe you should wake up your traveling companions and go check it out. How does that sound?"

I didn't even wait to answer him. I ran out of the kitchen and up the stairs to wake up my three friends.

I guess I should tell you a little about myself and how I got to Hollywood from my little hometown of Carverville. My name is Kyle Conlon. Uncle Rex called my dad and asked if I could visit over Christmas vacation. My uncle is a big-time TV producer. He produced a lot of the hits from last season. Every time he calls my dad, he tells him about the latest big movie star he's worked with. Uncle Rex knows a lot of Hollywood's famous people. But the great thing about my uncle is that it doesn't go to his head. He always says God has really blessed him and he has a lot to be thankful for.

Uncle Rex was working on a new TV show and needed a few teens to screen some of the early film clips. Uncle Rex wanted "regular" kids from the Midwest. Carverville is about as Midwest as a town can get. We've got corn everywhere. And next to the corn there are cows. Yes, Carverville is the Midwest.

I asked my three best friends, Brent, Sammy, and Sara, to come along. My uncle's film studio paid for our plane tickets and sent a big black limo to pick us up at the airport. The limo had a small refrigerator, filled with health food and carrot juice. Dad warned me that California was different from Carverville. I began to understand what he meant after I saw the foods in the limo.

During the ride from the airport to my uncle's house, Sammy was preoccupied with the buttons and gadgets in the limo. Brent looked around for movie stars. Sara and I looked at the trees and neat buildings. California didn't look anything like Carverville. The palm trees and flowering bushes made everything around us seem so fresh and beautiful. And the temperature outside was warm even though it was December. I was going to like California.

When we arrived at Uncle Rex's house, Sara's mouth dropped open. The house was bigger than any we had seen back home. The entrance hallway of the house was bigger than my parents' living room. Sammy got into trouble before our suitcases were even on the shiny marble floor.

The staircase was very long, and it had a winding railing along it. The railing was perfect for sliding down. The temptation got to Sammy before I could. Suddenly, I heard a cry that sounded something like a cowboy getting wounded by a stray bullet.

"You got me, buckaroo," Sammy called out to make sure that we all noticed him.

"Sammy, don't do that! This isn't your house. My aunt will kill us if she catches you," I scolded.

It was too late. Aunt Janet had already walked into the entryway. The sound of her shoes on the marble made me spin around quickly.

"That's all right, Kyle. It's been so long since kids played on that railing that I am glad to see someone using it the proper way," she said.

Sara leaned over and whispered in my ear, "This is going to be fun. Your aunt is really cool."

Aunt Janet continued, "Kyle, Uncle Rex won't be home from the TV studio till later. I'll make us some dinner and then we can go swimming in the pool."

Aunt Janet made us something to eat, showed us around the house, and led us to our bedrooms. My room was on the side of the house that overlooked an empty field next to some large warehouses.

When my aunt finally led us to the pool, we were awestruck. It was the biggest pool we had ever seen! Half of the pool was inside the house and the other half was outside. A wall of glass separated the inside from the outside. We jumped into the pool inside the house, swam under the glass wall, and came up outside the house. It was nothing like the public pool we had in Carverville.

Uncle Rex came home while we were swimming. My uncle was very tall, and his black hair was starting to turn gray. Dad sometimes kidded him about that. Uncle Rex usually retorted that at least he still had hair.

It was really great to see Uncle Rex. He had brought home a videotape of a scary movie that was going to hit the theaters in a few weeks. That impressed Sammy. We changed into dry clothes and went to the family room to watch the movie on the big-screen TV.

When the movie ended it was late, and we all went sleepily off to bed. The movie must have affected my dreams. In the middle of the night I had a frightening nightmare. In it, the four of us from Carverville were trapped inside a gigantic cuckoo clock with a time bomb. The seconds ticked away, bringing us closer to the explosion. The scream woke me up before the bomb could explode.

I couldn't believe that my friends had slept through that scream, but they had. My room was the only one on the side of the house next to the carnival. I guess that's why I heard it and they didn't.

I banged on Sammy's door. "Sammy, hurry up and get out of there. You won't believe this!"

Brent and Sara heard me pound on Sammy's door, and all three came into the hallway. "Come on," I said with a grin, "I've got to show you something. This is really cool."

We raced into my room and hurried over to look out the window. "Uncle Rex said that this carnival rented the field next door to his house and maybe we should go check it out. Is everybody up for it?" I asked.

Sammy, Sara, and I had already turned away from the window when we heard Brent scream. When I turned back around, I saw a gigantic, monstrous face pressed against the bedroom window.

Sara was on the floor. I thought she was having a panic attack until I listened to the noises she was making. She was laughing. I looked at the face in the window. It was a balloon that had floated up from the carnival. I had never seen one that had a monster's face painted on it.

Sammy said, "Hey, if the balloons can scare us that bad, maybe the rides can give us some good scares too." He enjoyed being scared. To Sammy, being scared was a way to know that you were a living, breathing human being. That wasn't my favorite thing, but I had to admit that the carnival looked like a great time. Both Aunt Janet and Uncle Rex had to work. Going to the carnival would definitely be more exciting than hanging around the house all day with the housekeeper, even if the house did have a pool, a big-screen TV, and dozens of movies to watch.

It only took us a half hour to shower, get dressed, and make it to the breakfast table. My aunt knew we wanted to get to the carnival quickly. She already had sweet rolls, juice, and cereal on the table. Brent and Sammy started to eat before Sara and I even sat down. I had just poured cereal into my bowl when Aunt Janet walked into the room.

"Aunt Janet, thanks for breakfast. We can't wait to get to the carnival."

A big smile spread across her face. "Have a great time. If I wasn't scheduled to be in L.A. for a meeting, I would join you. It looks like a lot of fun. If you need anything, the housekeeper will be here all day."

We gulped down our food and headed for the door. Aunt Janet caught me by the arm as I was walking out. "You might need some of this. Rex left it for you before going to the studio." She handed me some money. I couldn't believe that I almost forgot money! I gave Aunt Janet a hug and then ran to catch up with the others.

I ran so fast that I didn't notice that the others had stopped dead in their tracks. I slid to a halt in the gravel in front of the carnival gate. My three friends were staring up at it.

"What's up?" I asked.

Sammy pointed to the banner across the top of the gate. "DR. SHIVERS' CARNIVAL OF TERROR," it read. Sammy looked at me. "Awesome," he said.

"Not a very inviting name, is it?" Brent gulped as he spoke.

Sammy started to walk toward the gate as he answered Brent. "This looks like a great place to spend the day. California is way cool. You'd never see anything like this back in our little town."

"We've got some great stuff there too," Sara retorted.

"Like what?" Sammy laughed. "The last big thing that happened in Carverville was when the baptistry flooded at the church and Pastor Christensen had to wear wading boots when he gave the sermon." Just a reminder of that day made us all laugh.

"So why are we just standing here?" Brent asked. "Let's go explore!"

Everyone walked through the gate except for me. I was a little uneasy about this place. After all, the carnival had appeared so quickly and mysteriously. And there was that scream that woke me up. But what really got to me was the banner on the gate. I called the other three back to me so we could talk.

"Maybe we better think this through. You know, it doesn't really look like they're ready for customers. I'm thinking that it might be better if we went back to the house," I said nervously.

Sammy gave me his you've-got-to-be-kidding look, and then he said, "Time out. What are you talking about? You were the first one to want to come over here. I'm all excited and ready to go."

"I'm just thinking about your safety. Remember, I

invited all of you out here to California with me. If something happens to any of you, your parents will kill me. I'm not sure that an amusement park called Dr. Shivers' Carnival of Terror is safe," I argued.

Sara chimed in next. "Am I hanging out with a bunch of scaredy-cats? Let's just go in. If for some reason we get afraid of anything, we can leave. I mean what can they do, lock us in there?"

"Have a mummy chase us through a tomb?" Brent added, pointing out the silliness of my fear.

"All right. I guess I'm being a little too careful. What can it hurt?" I told them, hoping we weren't being foolish. I prayed a silent prayer asking the Lord to protect us. He'd been doing a lot of that lately. It seems the four of us have a way of getting ourselves into tough spots. And I had a feeling that this was going to be one of them.

The four of us went through the gate one at a time. Since I was the least eager one in the bunch, I was the last one through. My shoes had shuffled only a few steps from the gate when I was stopped by an eerie realization. Nobody else was there. No families. No kids. No workers. No one. Maybe *we* shouldn't be here either. At that moment, a wicked laugh came from behind me and a bony hand gripped my shoulder. I let out a scream.

We all spun around. I stared up into the long, sharp-featured face of a man. A thin mustache connected to a goatee gave the man's face a sinister look. On the top of his head sat a top hat like Abraham Lincoln wore. My jaw dropped open as I scanned the rest of the guy's clothing. He wore a tuxedo jacket, the kind with tails on it. It seemed very weird to me but, then again, this was California. The man's dark eyes stared down at me, and my mouth went dry.

"Can I help you, my young friends?" he asked slowly. His voice sounded like he was deep inside a barrel. It sent a tingle up my spine. Even his eyes were spooky. He opened them wide at first and then squinted at me. When his eyes popped open, his eyebrows raised and then they dropped as he squinted.

Sammy jumped right in. "We're staying with Kyle's uncle. He's a TV producer and he lives next door. When we woke up and saw the carnival, we wanted to be your first customers." He talked so fast that his words almost ran together.

"And that you are. But I'm afraid we're not open yet. There is still much work to be done." The man smiled at us as he spoke. "Oh, I'm sorry. I forgot to introduce myself. I am Dr. Shivers, the owner of this little traveling carnival. It is my distinct pleasure to welcome you."

I finally found my voice. "Nice to meet you, sir. When will you be open?"

"Not until tomorrow. I do hope you can come back then. I'm sure you're dying to try the carnival's amusements, games, and rides," he said. I didn't like how he said the word *dying*. I was kind of relieved that we couldn't stay.

We started to head for the gate when he called to us. "On second thought, kids, wait a moment. I've got some new rides and games. I would truly love it if you would test out my slight amusements, as we here at the carnival call our little rides and *harmless* games."

"Wow, yeah. That would be great! Like I was saying to my friends, nothing like this happens back in our little town." Sammy was nearly jumping up and down with excitement.

"Would you be so kind as to follow me back to my office and I'll give you special free admission passes that will allow you unpaid access to all of my amusements except for one, Dracula's Castle. It isn't quite finished yet. Dracula's coffin hasn't arrived from Transylvania. In case you didn't know, it has to sit on dirt from that country. When the Transylvanians sent the dirt, I told them, 'Fangs very much.'" He laughed with eerie glee at his own joke and then continued, "There's just so much to do in a carnival like this. So please, go ahead and enjoy yourselves as my guests, my very special guests. But I do have one request of you," he said.

Brent spoke first, "Sure. What can we do?"

"When you're done, that is when you feel like you're just about *dead* from exhaustion, return to my office and tell me what you think of my little carnival of terror," Dr. Shivers answered. I nodded my head that we would. I was not sure I ever wanted to see him again, but a promise was a promise.

Dr. Shivers motioned for us to follow him. We slipped between some tents and amusements. I looked at the names on the games and rides. There were some very strange things at this carnival.

His office was in a dented trailer. His picture was painted on the side, along with the words DR. SHIVERS' CARNIVAL OF TERROR. The painting was faded as if it had been in the sun for a lot of years.

Dr. Shivers opened the door and I walked inside. The room was filled with odd items. It looked like the set of a science fiction movie. A big stuffed raven stood on a perch in the corner of the office. At least, I think it was stuffed. For a moment I was sure the bird winked at me.

Dr. Shivers gave each of us a small skeleton on a necklace. But it wasn't an ordinary skeleton. It had the face of our bizarre Dr. Shivers on the skull. He told us to show them at any ride or refreshment stand and we could have what we wanted for free. Sammy was right. Nothing like this would ever happen back in our hometown.

Dr. Shivers gave us one last twisted smile before we left. As we walked away from his office I heard him laugh, and something told me that this carnival wasn't going to be all fun and games. I started to feel like it might indeed be filled with terror. There was definitely something sinister about his laugh. I closed my eyes for another quick prayer. *Lord, I know I can't go anywhere without You. Watch over us here and protect us from anything evil.*

Brent walked toward the right side of the midway, and Sammy and Sara headed down the left. I decided to join Brent. I was amazed. These were the strangest rides and games I had ever seen. I was sure that the others felt the same way. Friends could sense things like that.

Brent, Sammy, and Sara were my best friends. Brent and I had met a few months ago at the new church my family started going to. I liked hanging out with him. He is a little smaller than most of the kids our age. I supposed some of the others at middle school might have picked on him except that he's a great guy. Everyone likes him. He really cares about people.

Sara's dad is the pastor of our church. She loves baseball and has an impressive pitching arm. Her dark brown hair is straight and hangs to her shoulders, but most of the time she pulls it back in a ponytail. The most interesting thing about her is how she lives out her Christianity. It's not like she's trying to live up to the reputation of being a preacher's kid. It's more like she lives what she believes.

Sammy makes life just plain fun. Everything is an adventure to him. Sammy was born in Mexico, and his family later moved to Texas. His dad's a Roadway engineer, and his company transferred him to a city near Carverville a couple of years ago. Sammy's the kind of guy who jumps right into whatever comes along. Unfortunately, he has one drawback. He plays too many practical jokes on us. A place like Dr. Shivers' Carnival of Terror was ripe for Sammy's sense of humor.

Brent and I walked by two rides that sat on top of mobile trailers. As we were looking around, Brent said, "You know, Dr. Shivers looks familiar. There was something about his eyes. He reminded me of a guy I saw on TV."

I scoffed, "Come on, Brent, a guy like Dr. Shivers would never be on TV. He's probably traveled all over the world with this carnival. Besides, if you saw him before, it was probably a picture on a 'Wanted' poster in the post office. He looked like a pretty rough character to me."

"No, he seemed okay. I know I've seen him, and if I keep thinking about it, it will come to me," he insisted.

While we were talking someone called to us. "Hey, kids. Come on, try your luck in the Gremlins' Shooting Gallery. Three bull's-eyes and you can win a teddy bear. What do you say, kids? Give it a try. Impress your friends with your skill." The words came from a man standing in front of a shooting gallery.

I laughed and looked at Brent. "I thought this was a carnival of terror. This is like something you'd see at a carnival back home. Let's try to find something a little more exciting."

The guy yelled to us again, "Try the Gremlins' Gallery. Don't be chicken!"

"Who's a chicken?" said a voice from behind us. I spun around and Sammy and Sara were standing there. "We're not chickens. What's there to be afraid of in a shooting gallery?" Sara responded.

"I'm sorry, kids. I thought I was talking to a gang of middle schoolers. This might be too frightening for you," the man by the gallery taunted Sara.

"I'm going in. Anybody joining me?" Sara called as she walked forward. Normally, Sara felt pretty sure of herself and didn't have to prove anything. But we weren't quite ourselves in this place and were ready to take a dare. We fell in line behind her.

"Just follow the stairs up to the gallery and walk down the hall, folks," the guy instructed as we entered.

The stairway got darker as we neared the top. When we reached the hall, the others started goofing around, and I moved to the front of the line. I bumped into a wall at the end of the hallway, then Sammy bumped into me, and Brent and Sara bumped into Sammy.

Sammy yelled, "Hey, this hallway ended. Where do we go now?"

"If it doesn't go anywhere then maybe we need to turn around and go back," Sara suggested. She had barely gotten the words out of her mouth when a panel slid across the hallway behind us, sealing us inside.

"Hey, what is this? What's happening? I can't see a thing," I yelled.

"Attention please. Welcome to the Gremlins' Shooting Gallery. In a moment the wall before you will open, and you will have three seconds to seek cover before the gremlins begin shooting. And remember, if they hit three of you, you win a teddy bear . . . that is, if you're still around to collect your prize." The voice came from a speaker above us.

"I'm scared, Kyle," Brent whispered.

"It's a joke. It's got to be a joke. Don't you think, Sammy?" I asked.

"Of course it is," Sammy said fearlessly.

Then the wall slid open. This was no joke after all. Before us was a group of large wooden ducks, and on the other side of the shooting gallery counter stood a bunch of gremlins. Their beady eyes peered through the scopes on their water rifles as they stood there cackling.

The voice from the speaker screamed with urgency, "Your three seconds are up. Take cover!"

I heard pumping and then streams of water shot toward us. We were the targets in a wet shooting gallery.

I dived behind one of the ducks. Sammy and Sara were right behind me. In the dim light I could see them crouching to take cover. Then Brent screamed in mock terror: "I've been hit."

I dived from behind the large wooden duck and slid across the wet floor to Brent's feet. I regained my footing and grabbed him by the waist, pulling him down. He fell next to me.

"How do we get out of here?" he whispered, giggling.

"I don't know. I think the doors have sealed us in. Sammy, Sara, are you all right?" I called to them.

"What's going on? This is crazy," Sara laughed back over the sound of water streams splashing.

"Sara, crawl back toward the wall and see if you can get the doors open. But stay down so you don't get soaked," I told her.

Sammy asked, "Brent, are you okay?"

"Yeah, the water just surprised me," he answered.

"Sara, did you find anything yet?" I called.

"Nothing. This door is sealed off tight. Try the wall by you, and I'll try the one by me."

As long as we stayed low or behind the wooden

ducks we were safe. The gremlins were just tall enough to reach the water rifles. They couldn't aim their rifles downward unless they were on the counter separating us. I crawled low to the ground all the way to the side wall. I pushed and kicked the wall. I even rubbed it. Nothing. There wasn't even a seam dividing the pieces of wood. We were sealed inside.

I kicked the wall again and then felt a stream of water hit just above my head. I spun around. The gremlins had figured it out. They were crawling onto the counter.

"Kyle, get back behind the ducks. The gremlins are on the counter. They could nail you. Sara, do the same thing," Sammy yelled to us.

"Heading back now," Sara responded as she took a headlong dive toward the ducks. She landed next to Sammy. I saw what she did and imitated it. Sara and Sammy were behind one duck and Brent and I were behind another. We were stuck. There didn't appear to be a way out.

The water started hitting the ducks harder. The force of the spray was soaking us even behind the ducks. The gremlins had changed weapons. Now they each had something that looked and felt more like a fire hose. The force of the water would knock us down if we didn't stay behind the ducks.

"Ouch! This isn't fun anymore," Sara shouted after nearly being knocked across the room.

I was getting angry too, and worried. "What now? Any ideas?" I asked.

"Anybody up for an old-fashioned prayer meeting?" Sammy joked to relieve our frustration at being trapped. I figured even he had to be scared now.

But I didn't have time to feel any relief because other gremlins were climbing onto the counter. The situation was getting worse. Water was several inches deep everywhere.

"Sammy, how many gremlins are on the counter now?" Sara asked.

Sammy carefully peeked around the corner of the duck. The moment his eyes moved to the edge of the duck, water exploded against the wall behind him. "I didn't have time to count, but it must be all of them, and I think they've sent out for more friends."

"I wish they'd send out for pizza and leave us alone." Brent crossed his arms over his chest and sank deeper behind the duck as he spoke.

"We'll get out, Brent," Sammy encouraged. "And we'll certainly have an earful of feedback for Dr. Shivers."

"Shooting at us isn't good for customer loyalty," Brent chirped in.

We all laughed.

Just then I heard the sound of padded, clawed feet hitting the floor. The gremlins were jumping off the counter. Not even the ducks could protect us now.

21

As the gremlins moved toward us, I held my breath.
More than anything, I wished we could get out of this
place. I also wished I'd listened to my instincts and
not come in the first place.

"Do you hear that?" Brent whispered to me.

"The gremlins," I answered.

"No, that humming noise. I can feel a vibration
underneath the floor. What's going on?"

The floor moved. It started to tilt. I tried to hold on
to a duck, but the floor's tilt increased by the second.
Soon Sammy and Sara banged into Brent and me,
and the four of us slid toward the wall. We were
going to smack right into it.

The gremlins were screaming behind us. Their
section of the floor hadn't tilted. I saw them jumping
up and down in frustration. We slid closer to the
wall. In a few seconds we would crash into it.

We hit the wall and went through it. The tilted
floor had exposed a section of black plastic wall that

wasn't attached at the bottom. We slid out into the daylight and fell on air mattresses next to the amusement's side wall.

"That was great!" Sammy yelled. "This place is fantastic. What do we do next?"

"Next? I think we ought to get out of here," I said. "We could have really been hurt in there."

"Come on, it was just a game. I mean, we got out of there, right? Besides, we just got here. This place could be a lot of fun. Let's try another one, just to see."

"Sammy's right. Let's try something else. What else do we have to do? And don't forget that Dr. Shivers is counting on us to give him some feedback," Brent said.

"Hey, what's this?" Sara asked as she reached down and picked up what looked like a marble. As she rolled it around in her hand, I realized what she had.

"It's an eye!" I gasped.

"Let me see that," Brent said as he snatched it from her hand. "Yep, it's an eye all right," he stated matter-of-factly. He suddenly realized what he'd said. He yelled and tossed the eyeball into the air. Sammy caught it as it fell.

"It's only a marble that looks like an eye," he observed.

"What's it doing here?" I asked.

"I guess someone is keeping an eye out for us," Sammy responded.

Sara interrupted our snickers, "I think it's a clue."

"A clue to what?" Sammy asked with a doubtful look.

"I think she's right," I told them. "Maybe it will make sense later. Let's go check out more of this carnival."

Sammy agreed and headed for the Shoot the Chute. It was a very tall structure with a series of inflated plastic tubes that branched off the center. The whole thing looked like a really tall spider with a dozen legs. The tubes ran all over the place. Some to the front, some to the back, and a few even stretched to other parts of the carnival. I had to admit it looked like fun.

A long stairway led to the top. We ran up the first twenty steps. Brent and I took the rest of the stairs a little slower. I was panting by the time I reached the top. I collapsed next to Brent, who had already sat down to catch his breath.

Sammy and Sara stood on the platform. They scanned the tube openings, trying to decide which ones they would choose.

"Sara, this is great," Sammy said. "Hey guys, each tube has a name on it. This one is The Devil's Doorway, and this one is The Twister."

"Do they have one called Tube to Oblivion? That's where I'm going if I can ever stand up again. My legs feel like rubber," I joked.

Sara said seriously, "That's why I'm choosing the longest tube I can find. I want to sit for a few minutes." Sara chose a tube, climbed inside, and started to slide. We could hear her yelling, "This is fantastic," the whole way down.

Sammy picked The Twister and hopped in. He hollered, "Yabba dabba doo," as he slid down. Sammy watched way too much TV when he was a little kid.

"I'm taking The Lizard's Leap," Brent said. He dropped out of sight.

I was glad that the others had already gone down. I didn't want anyone to see me when I plopped my legs inside the tube marked Soft and Smooshy. It sounded like something for little kids. That was okay with me. All I wanted was a rest and no weird twists and turns.

I slid down, then shot upward, and then downward again. A few times I bounced off the rubbery plastic sides and spun around in the tube. This was fun! I wished now that I had taken one of the other tubes so the ride would have lasted longer. I was really enjoying myself. At least, that's what I thought until my tube ride ended.

I expected to land on the ground outside the Shoot the Chute. Instead, I dropped a few feet into a spongy, slippery, gooey mess. It was definitely soft and smooshy. The more I struggled to get out, the deeper I sank. I was inside something, but I didn't know what that something was. It was pitch black. What now? I prayed and yelled for help.

At the exact moment I yelled, something crashed into the goo next to me. I heard it thud, then thrash around. Whatever it was, it fell too close for my comfort.

I screamed. It screamed back.

"Sara, is that you?" I asked with relief.

"Yeah, it's me. But where are we?" I could tell from her voice that she was shaken up by the goo.

"I don't know, but if you keep moving around in this stuff, you'll sink both of us. Stand still for a second," I told her. Each time she moved I could feel her sinking deeper. When she grabbed on to me, I started to sink as well. We had to get out.

"Kyle, have you tried calling for help?" Sara asked.

A few seconds before you got here," I said, desperately looking for a way out. "Sara, we need to do this slowly. Let's each walk in a different direction until we reach the wall. We must be inside the Shoot the Chute. There has got to be a wall at the edge. Maybe we can punch through it or go under it."

We moved in opposite directions. It was hard pushing my body through the goo. It didn't seem wet, but my feet and legs worked very hard with each step. I made a mental note not to tell our gym teacher, Ms. Megamuscle Moreno, about this stuff. She'd install one of these pits at the middle school.

"Kyle, I reached the wall," Sara said.

"Good, I think I'm almost there too," I called back.

"I'm touching the wall now. I feel a rope," she said. "Don't pu—"

I was too late. She had already pulled it. At Dr. Shivers' Carnival of Terror you didn't want to do anything that could make things worse. A gremlin could drop through one of those tubes next.

"What's that sound, Kyle?"

We heard a hissing. It sounded like air escaping from a tire—a huge tire, like they use on those monster pickup trucks.

I screamed to Sara, "Quick, go back to the middle. This place is starting to deflate. We'll be crushed by the walls."

I heard Sara huffing and groaning as she sloshed through the goo. I moved toward her sounds and she moved toward mine. The hissing grew louder. I could almost feel the heavy plastic sagging around us.

Then the walls collapsed. I closed my eyes and waited.

I heard laughing.

I opened my eyes and saw that the Shoot the Chute had collapsed all around us and we were standing in the warm California sun again. Sammy and Brent were laughing at us.

"What are you guys laughing at?" Sara asked.

"You two," Sammy said. "How did you get in there and why were your eyes closed? You look like you expected the world to come to an end."

"Close enough. Help us out of here," I responded.

Sara stopped me. She was still holding the rope she'd pulled. At the end of it was a tea bag. "Kyle, why is there a tea bag on this rope?"

"It must be clue number two," I said.

"Clue to what?" Brent asked.

"I don't know. I just know that we have an eye and a tea bag," I answered.

"An eye and a tea—wait a second! That could be it! Maybe the two represent the letters *I* and *T*," Sammy said.

"This is really strange," Sara added. "I think I'm ready for a more normal ride."

"How about the merry-go-round? Maybe a kiddy ride will be just the ticket," Sammy mocked as he helped pull Sara and me out of the goo.

In truth, I disagreed with Sammy. I'd thought soft and smooshy would be a safe and easy ride. We had asked the Lord to protect us and He had. Now we were running headlong into who knew what else. *Were we going from trusting God to testing God?*

Sara and I headed to the restrooms to wash off the

goo. Then we followed the others to the merry-go-round. Brent was the first one on. He seemed really happy to find a ride that couldn't hurt us, splash us, or dump us in goo. Sammy bounded onto the biggest horse he could find. Sara and I climbed onto the two smaller horses between Sammy's and Brent's. The merry-go-round started slowly. I didn't see an operator, but that didn't surprise me. Everything at Dr. Shivers' carnival was a little strange.

"Hey look, a brass ring," Sammy called to us.

He was trying to reach it. It was too far away from me, so I didn't try. On the third time around, I read the sign over it. It said, DON'T PULL THE BRASS RING.

I yelled to Sammy, "The sign says 'Don't pull the—'" But it was too late. His finger slipped inside the ring and grabbed it. Out it came.

"I got it!" he said triumphantly.

I was about to tell him what the sign said and that he was crazy when the merry-go-round started to speed up. Sammy thought it was great fun, but I saw fear on Brent's face. Each second it spun faster and faster.

I started to climb off my horse and reach for Brent when the wooden pony bucked me. I grabbed for the neck of the horse and held on. Soon all the horses were bucking.

"Hold on. It looks like we're in for a wild ride," Sara said.

Our horses bucked up and down as the carousel spun faster and faster. I was getting dizzy and could barely hold on.

I gripped the horse's neck tighter, but each time it bucked it loosened my grip. I went a few inches into the air. I noticed some letters were branded into the leather reins of my horse. The bucking made it hard to read them.

PULL— I read, but the horse bucked me into the air before I could finish reading.

PULL BACK— I read when I landed on the horse. Then another buck sent me a few inches higher. The merry-go-round was spinning faster. I didn't have much time.

PULL BACK ON THE— I noticed Sara was slipping off her horse. The force of the spinning carousel would soon throw her into the midway.

PULL BACK ON THE REINS— The wooden animal tossed me a few inches higher that time.

PULL BACK ON THE REINS HARD— I needed to stay seated long enough to read all the words, but the up-and-down motion and the spinning made it very difficult. Sammy looked like he was having a great time.

PULL BACK ON THE REINS HARD TO— To what? What happens when I pull back hard on the reins? I had to find out. The next buck of the horse dropped me hard. I slipped sideways on the horse. I struggled back into the saddle just before the next toss hit me. This time I had to hold on and read the letters.

PULL BACK ON THE REINS HARD TO STOP, it read.

"Everybody, pull back hard on your reins. It will stop the merry-go-round," I yelled. They did as I said. The carousel started to slow. The bucking stopped, and soon the merry-go-round came to a halt.

I let out a long sigh. Brent and Sara did the same, but Sammy had jumped down from his horse and was running into the midway. He looked at us and motioned for us to follow him. "What do we go on next?" he asked. The three of us staggered off the carousel with our heads spinning from the wild ride.

"Next, we go home," Brent shot back.

"Not yet," Sara called. "I want to look for more clues."

I was curious too. I turned back toward the carousel. Looking up at the horses, I stopped. I couldn't believe it. The clue was all over the place.

"Sara, look at the brand on the horses," I called.

"*S*!" she answered. "We have an *I*, a *T*, and an *S*. That spells *its*, but what does that mean?"

"I don't know. All I know is that there's nothing like this back in our little town. I want to keep going." Sammy was pleading. I thought if he put down "our little town" one more time, I was going to scream.

"Look," he said, "there's a Ferris wheel. We can get high enough to look down on the whole carnival. Then we'll pick out a couple of safe-looking rides that Dr. Shivers can't turn into something that will give you a heart attack. How about it?"

"Okay, but if we don't see anything then that's it. We go back to Kyle's uncle's house." Brent was insistent.

We staggered to the Ferris wheel and jammed ourselves in a bucket. After I sat down I looked up. I shouldn't have because every time I saw a sign around this place it scared me. This one read, THE FEAR-US WHEEL.

"This isn't a Ferris wheel," I said. My three friends stared back at me like I had lost some of my brains on the merry-go-round. "Look, the good doctor calls this a *Fear-Us Wheel.* I think we should get out before something crazy happens on this thing."

I spoke too late. The safety bar snapped down on us, making it impossible to get out. A glass cage covered the front and sides of the bucket. We started to move.

At first it was just the slow, usual circular movements of a Ferris wheel. The others made fun of my concern. We looked out of the glass for other rides we wanted to go on.

I still didn't trust this place. I wished my aunt or uncle would come get us for some reason. Any reason would be good. I didn't want my friends to think I was chicken, but this place was spooky.

The Fear-Us Wheel bucket was rounding the top when it stopped. "I warned you guys, but nobody ever listens to me," I mumbled, using my best I-told-you-so voice.

"It'll start again. Someone else must be getting on," Sara said hopefully.

"Like who? The Munsters?" I scoffed.

The Fear-Us Wheel swayed from side to side. My stomach was getting upset. I think I discovered what seasickness felt like.

"What do we do now?" Brent asked.

"Wait. All we can do is wait and see what Dr. Shivers has up his sleeve," Sara answered.

"Spiders," Sammy said.

"Dr. Shivers has spiders up his sleeve?" Sara was puzzled.

"No, there are spiders on our Fear-Us Wheel bucket." He said it like he was answering a teacher's question. He was very calm. Brent wasn't.

"Don't say that. I really hate spiders. I mean, *really*."
Brent covered his eyes with his hands as he spoke.

"Brent, he's not kidding. There are spiders on the
outside of the glass. But in here we should be safe.
Besides, the four of us should be able to handle a
handful of spiders." As I said that, more and more
began to crawl onto the outside of the glass. In a
couple of minutes the glass was covered with spiders,
hundreds of them.

Brent opened his eyes and saw them. I thought he
was going to climb out of the bucket and jump. Sara
and I held him down.

"Don't look," Sara warned him.

"What do you mean, don't look! I'm in a nest of
spiders and you tell me not to look! I want to see
what is going to wrap me in its web and come back
to devour me! I'm going to be spider stew! Who is
going to explain to my mother that I was a snack for
a bunch of spiders? Someone get us out of here!"
he yelled.

We all started to scream for help. The bucket rocked back and forth. We swayed from side to side. I hoped the movement would shake off the spiders. It didn't affect them at all. They continued to crawl all over the glass. I was surprised that none got inside.

The swaying stopped. The Fear-Us Wheel began to move again. It slowly descended to the bottom. We stopped with a jolt, the safety bar flew up, the glass slid back, and we bolted from the ride.

"Keep the spiders away from me," Brent said.

I looked back. There wasn't a spider anywhere. Not on the ground, not on the bucket, and not on the glass. That was weird—very weird.

"What now?" Sammy was still optimistic that this place was great.

"I'm up for leaving, except there should be another clue," Sara said. Something hit her from behind. She spun around and watched an innertube flop to the ground.

"Oh, there's my clue."

"If that's a clue, then what does it mean?" Brent asked.

"It means that a big wave is going to crash into the carnival and we'll all need innertubes," Sammy joked.

"No, I think we've found another letter. It's the letter *O*," I told him.

"What is this, Sesame Street? Can we at least win a stuffed animal before we go?" Sammy asked.

It seemed like a reasonable request. Maybe it would help us forget the spiders. And besides, searching for clues was fun. Everything had turned out okay so far.

Sammy was the first one to the game booth. "All we've got to do is hit one of those two black dots with a ball. It looks easy enough."

"You three go ahead," Brent said. "I want to sit down. Spiders make me a little weak in the knees."

Sammy grabbed the first ball, wound up, and let the ball fly. It missed by a foot. He shrugged his shoulders and moved out of the way.

I took the next try. Baseball wasn't really my sport, and pitching was what I was the worst at. I probably would have done better if I had closed my eyes. At least I wouldn't have seen the ball miss the target by three feet. I did hit one of the stuffed animals on the shelf behind the targets.

"Do I get to keep what I hit?" I joked. I thought it was pretty funny, but the others just rolled their eyes.

"My turn," Sara said as she grabbed the ball. Sara was our last chance at winning. She was also our best chance. She pitched for our Little League team. Last year she even threw a no-hitter. She rubbed the ball and eyed one of the targets. Sara wound up, and the pitch was good. It struck right in the center of one of the black spots.

"You did it!" Brent yelled. "I knew you could, Sara."

"All those tips I gave you really worked," Sammy kidded.

"They're moving," I said nervously.

"What's moving, Kyle?" Sara asked.

"The black spots are moving. Look—they're starting to get higher." I pointed at the targets, and we saw two long antennae rise over the shelf. They were attached to a greenish, fish-scaled head. Long, jagged teeth appeared when the beast roared at us.

"Those weren't targets. They were eyes. And it is really mad!" Sammy yelled.

"Run for it," Brent yelled.

We turned around as the door to the carnival game began to slide shut. *Not again,* I thought. Sammy dived out and Sara was only inches behind him. I pushed Brent as the sliding doors got closer and closer.

Sara saw a pole leaning against the outside wall of the ball-toss game. She grabbed it and wedged the pole between the sliding doors. It stopped them, and she and Sammy pulled Brent through.

I dived for the opening. I had just cleared it when a slimy hand grabbed my leg. I felt the scales and the claws wrap tight around my calf.

"It's got me! It's going to pull me back in!" I yelled. I figured that I was going to be this green sea monster's mid-morning snack. I tried kicking its hand away, but this refugee from the sea was too strong.

Sammy jumped up to see what he could do. His

head bumped the pole holding the doors open and knocked it loose. The doors continued to slide together until they closed on the monster's arm. I heard it moan, and then it let go of me.

This place was weirder than I imagined. I lay on the ground breathing a sigh of relief when something moved between me and the sun. It was a shadow. I turned my head to see what it was.

A clown stood over us. He honked his horn. I think he was saying hello. Everybody turned when they heard the horn.

"Hey, it's a clown," exclaimed Sara.

"Brilliant deduction, Sherlock," Sammy mocked.

"Maybe he can tell us about this place. Mr. Clown, sir, we've run into some very weird stuff around here. What's behind all this?" Brent asked.

The clown didn't answer. He reached deep into his pants pocket and pulled out a coin. He held it in one hand and then grabbed it with the other. The clown waved the empty open hand over the one with the coin in it, beeped his horn, and then opened his hand. The coin was gone.

He walked over to me, reached behind my ear, and took out the coin. He never said a word.

Sara looked puzzled. She turned to us and said, "I think he was trying to tell us something. The trick means something."

"Oh, good, we're all going to disappear and then

41

reappear in Kyle's ear. That's comforting." Sammy laughed as he spoke.

"Let me ask him another question." Sara turned again to the clown. "Are you an important person at the carnival?"

"Why ask him something stupid like that? He's just a clown," Sammy tossed in.

The clown ignored Sammy's comment and reached into his pocket again. He pulled out a large, red cloth with his left hand and draped it over his right. He held his right hand in front of him with his palm up. He passed his left hand over the cloth three times, beeped his horn, and grabbed the cloth. When he lifted it, he had a flower in his hand.

We applauded.

Sammy turned to Sara and asked, "Okay, so what does a flower have to do with his being important?"

"I get it," Brent said. "The flower is a forget-me-not. I guess we shouldn't forget him."

"I think it will be hard to forget anything around this place," I said. "I've got another question. Are we in danger here? What will happen if we stay?"

The clown smiled and pulled the coin from his pocket again. He tossed it to me and walked away. I stared at him and then at the coin. Scratched on one side was the letter *N*. It was our clue, but on the other side of the coin there was a more important message: "In God We Trust."

"I'm getting hungry," Sammy said. "Anyone else want something to eat?"

We walked to a food stand. Inside the stand, an older woman gave us a big smile and said, "I see you're wearing the special necklaces. Can I get you kids something compliments of Dr. Shivers?"

Sammy answered, "Sure, I want a hot dog."

She grabbed one from the shelf behind her. It was wrapped in foil.

"And what can I get you?" the vendor asked with a big smile.

"Cotton candy, please," Brent responded. Maybe fear gave Brent a sweet tooth. Neither Sara nor I wanted anything. I was just ready to go home.

The woman was very kind. Her smile gave me hope that Dr. Shivers' Carnival of Terror was not all bad. As we turned to walk away, the woman closed the refreshment stand.

Sammy bit into his hot dog and it barked. We all turned and looked at him.

"It wasn't me," he said. "My hot dog barked."

"Sure it did," Sara scoffed.

"It did. Listen." He bit into the hot dog again. It barked. Sara started laughing. Sammy then caught the giggles, and when he laughs it doesn't take long until he's on the ground. I was walking over to look at the hot dog when I heard Brent scream.

"There are worms in my cotton candy! My cotton candy is filled with worms!" He dropped it.

Brent hopped up and down, shaking his hands in the air. The worms really grossed him out. Sara and I nearly bumped heads reaching down to pick up the cotton candy. Sammy was still laughing. His barking hot dog had struck him so funny that he couldn't stop. Sara grabbed the cotton candy first, scooped it up, and checked it out. The worms freaked her out too.

"Come on, I want to see too," I said in frustration. This carnival kept getting weirder by the minute.

Sara gagged and turned her head away from the pink spun sugar. "You don't really."

"I do," I snapped. I grabbed the paper cone of cotton candy by its point. I didn't want to get worms on me. When I tipped it up and looked inside, I saw worms creeping and crawling up the paper. It was gross.

I looked at Brent. "Did you eat any of it?"

"Yes," he gagged out.

Sammy was still laughing. "At least you got some protein with every bite."

"That's not funny, Sammy," Brent shot back.

"Hold it, now. We can't get mad at each other. We're supposed to be having fun here," I said as I moved between the two.

"If you think eating worms is fun, then I'm having a ball," Brent said, and then he broke out in giggles. He realized how ridiculous we sounded. My laughter followed. At first I only giggled, then it grew into full-fledged belly laughs.

Sammy stopped laughing long enough to stand up to see the cotton candy. But when he looked at it he burst into laughter again, falling to the ground and holding his stomach. "Somebody stop me. It hurts."

Sara alternated between gagging and giggling. When Sara laughed she threw her head back in the air and let out the funniest and loudest laughs I ever heard.

"My hot dog barked," Sammy howled from the ground.

"And I had the cotton candy that ate Hollywood," Brent snorted out.

The laughter helped us relax. We sat up and then slowly got to our feet. Sammy was still on the ground and Sara reached her hand down to help him up. Sara looked at him and asked, "Don't you think there's a lot of weird stuff around here?"

"This could all be a dream," Sammy said.

"If this is a dream," I answered, "then someone pinch me."

No one pinched me.

Sara turned to us and said, "I forgot to look for another clue. So far we have *I, T, S, O,* and *N*."

"If you add an apostrophe between the *T* and *S*, it spells *it's on*," Brent added.

"I don't see anything," I said. "But I'd like to know what *it* is and what *it* is *on*. Let's keep looking."

I think my confidence in God's protection was growing with each event. Sometimes I need to be reminded that the Lord is always faithful. Dr. Shivers' carnival was reminding me over and over again.

We started to walk down the midway, looking at all the amusements and wondering what the next clue would be. None of us could explain what was going on, but Dr. Shivers' Carnival of Terror seemed to be living up to its name.

"It all seems a little fishy to me," Sara said. "I mean, think about it. Gremlins? Sea monsters? Barking hot dogs? These things can't be real, right?"

Sammy butted in, "And why did the spiders disappear when we got off the Fear-Us Wheel? I agree, there's something fishy going on."

"Then what do we do next?" I was ready for some answers.

Sara looked at me and said, "I say that we stay

here and figure out where this alphabet mystery is heading."

"Great," Sammy added, "then let's hit another ride." He looked around. We had reached the end of the midway. "Nothing's here. Let's head back the other way."

Brent stood in front of the last tent on the midway. "The sign says the next show is in two minutes. I could use a few minutes to sit down."

Sara and I shrugged our shoulders as if to say, "That's okay by us." I thought to myself, *It isn't a ride, a shooting gallery, or even food. It must be okay.* Sammy didn't want to see the show. He wanted to go on another ride. Brent, Sara, and I went into the tent without him and sat in the front.

The sign above the stage read, GREAT CHARACTERS OF ITERATURE. The *L* in *literature* was missing. Sara and I looked at each other. We had just discovered the next clue. It must be the *L*. This made me feel better about being there. I jabbed Sara in the ribs and whispered, "Who do you think they'll have from the world of literature? Or is that *iterature*?" I had no more than finished my question when a man in a white lab coat pushed clumsily through the curtains.

"You are about to witness some of the great experiments in our history. Behind this curtain is one of the marvels of the world," he said.

"First you will meet my associate, Dr. Jekyll. He has

created a new soft drink that is better than anything on the market today. It is the kind of drink that can change your life. It is so good that you won't be able to control yourself. You will want more and more. And now, here is Dr. Jekyll," the scientist told us.

The curtain opened to reveal Dr. Jekyll standing behind a lab table. Tubes ran everywhere, and different colored liquids pulsed through them. A bottle of bubbly, bluish liquid stood in the middle of the table.

"Most of us want to change something about ourselves. We either want to be taller or stronger, prettier or more outgoing. I have created a drink that makes you into what you want to be," the doctor lectured.

Sara leaned over and whispered, "So that's why Dr. Jekyll made his famous potion. And look what it did to him. I'm glad Jesus is my friend and is going to make me into what I want to be without stupid drinks and pills and hocus-pocus."

I knew she was right, but I leaned over to Brent and snickered. "Hey, Brent, I wish I'd had that last week at the football game. I wanted to be a tank to break through the other team's line. Do you think that I could be a tank if I drank that stuff?"

Brent laughed, and Dr. Jekyll glared at us.

"Hey, you two, I think you're making him mad," Sara said. "Just cool it! I don't want him to come out here after us."

I sat up straight in my seat and so did Brent. The doctor continued talking about his drink. I was getting a little bored and stopped watching just as the old guy raised the bottle to his lips. Then I heard Sara gasp.

I glanced at her, then looked back at the stage. Dr. Jekyll's body shook, and he jumped around the stage, screaming at the top of his voice. He raced from side to side, then off the side of the stage, then back on again. His appearance began to change.

Dropping to the floor, the doctor kicked his feet like he was having a temper tantrum. I leaned over to Brent and said, "Where are we? Baby-sitting your little brother?"

Brent laughed again. Bad move. Dr. Jekyll stood up. He had gone through a total transformation. A beastly set of eyes glared out of his twisted and distorted face. His crooked body stepped around the lab table and started our way. He dragged his limp left leg behind him.

I started to panic. He was almost to the edge of the stage when the curtains closed and stopped him.

"That was close," Brent sighed. Sara sighed too.

The man in the lab coat walked out from the stage wings and smiled at us. "I'm so sorry. My friend Dr. Jekyll can't always control his emotions when he is being heckled." He smirked at us and continued. "I am so sorry I forgot to introduce myself. I am Dr.

Frankenstein, and behind this curtain stands my creation."

The three of us looked at one another. This place had taken a wrong turn again. The curtains began to move a little, then a nonhuman voice cried out, "Argh!" The red velvet curtains drew open, and before us stood Frankenstein's monster.

Sara immediately stood up. "Quick, get out, get out!"

The monster was only a few rows away from us. He looked at us, then at Dr. Frankenstein.

The doctor tried to hold him back, but the monster swung his large arm at the doctor, knocking him to the stage. The monster headed toward us.

I turned to Brent and grabbed him by the arm. He was frozen with fear in his seat. Sara tried to get him to stand.

"Come on, Brent, let's get out of here," I yelled as I pulled him to his feet and out into the aisle. Sara pushed him and I pulled at him all the way to the exit doors.

As I reached the doors, all I could think about were the times that the doors to an amusement had slid shut on us. I prayed that this time the doors would be open.

I turned my head and saw that the monster was only a few feet behind us. *The doors have to open,* I thought.

My hand reached for the crash bar on the door. "Please, Lord, make them open," I prayed aloud. I pressed with all my weight against the metal door. Brent and Sara crashed against me.

I heard the monster's big feet thud on the ground right behind us. "Let's get out of—"

"He's got me!" Sara screamed.

I turned my head quickly. For a moment I forgot the door. Something happened in my head. The only thing I could think to do was to karate chop the monster's arm. I leaped in the air, gave my best kung fu scream, and came down hard on the arm.

"Ow!" I yelled. The monster felt like he was made of steel. I looked the monster in the eyes. He was shocked and let go of Sara's arm.

By then, Brent had pushed the door open and we went flying into the sunlight, stumbling and falling into the dirt of the midway. On the other side of the door, the monster yelled, "Why?" over and over again.

Sammy stood over us. "You guys didn't stay very long. Was the show that bad?"

I was breathing hard as I tried to explain. "A monster—Frankenstein—grabbed Sara—the door—"

Sammy's face beamed. "Wow! I can't believe I missed all that fun. I'm not sitting out one more thing around this place. Everything is better than what it seems. Let's go back inside."

"Everything is *weirder* than it seems, you mean," Sara said. "I'm not going back inside for anything."

Brent caught his breath and stepped between us. "Listen, I'm not sure I know what's going on, but I want to solve the mystery."

"We've already got the next two clues," Sara told him.

"I know about the *L*, but what's the next clue?" I asked with my puzzled, crunched-eyebrow look.

"What did Frankenstein yell?" Sara asked me.

"Why?" Sammy asked.

"That's it!" she exclaimed.

"That's what? Why do you care what Frankenstein yelled?" Sammy asked, confused.

That's when I jumped in. "I get it. The monster yelled *Why?* but it wasn't a question."

"It was the letter *Y*," Brent said as he realized what we were talking about.

"That means we have *I, T, S, O, N, L,* and *Y*. What does that spell?" Sara asked.

"What are we doing here, cheering for a basketball team or trying to solve a mystery?" Sammy joked.

"*It's only,*" I said. "It spells *It's only*. I wonder where the next clue will come from."

Sammy poked Brent and pointed. Brent's face lit up. "Look! There's a Tilt-a-Whirl over there. That's my favorite ride in the world. I'm going to go on it. I bet I've ridden Tilt-a-Whirls a hundred times. Nothing weird can happen there."

Brent marched toward the ride before I could stop

54

him. Dr. Shivers had been able to make everything else twice as frightening as it should be. I was sure that the Tilt-a-Whirl wouldn't be any different.

"Wait up, Brent. If you're going on that ride, we all are. From now on, we better hang together," I called after him.

The Tilt-a-Whirl is a basic spinning ride that rises and falls on small hills. Sometimes it goes really fast. I've always liked it too.

But everything at Dr. Shivers' Carnival of Terror was unpredictable. I thought about the merry-go-round. I had little hope that the Tilt-a-Whirl would be normal.

Brent was the first one on. Then Sammy and Sara climbed on. I looked around for spiders, Franken-stein's monster, barking hot dogs, or strange clowns. I didn't see anything or anybody, not even a person to run the ride. I cautiously got on.

When I sat down, the safety bar dropped and secured us in. The ride began to move slowly, then faster and faster.

"You would think that Dr. Shivers would come up with something different. We've already gone fast. We've already been trapped on rides," Sammy said with disappointment in his voice.

Then he startled us all by yelling, "Dr. Shivers, this ride isn't very frightening!"

"It will be!" came a voice from a loudspeaker.

"Thanks, Sammy. Thanks a lot," I said. "Now he's going to make this one more frightening than all the others."

The entire ride began to sink into the ground. It was lowered a foot every couple of seconds until we were in some kind of pit. Ghostly faces appeared along the walls of the pit. "I've got to get off this ride!" I screamed.

"Not now! The force of the spin will toss you like a rag doll. Stay in the car. I'll figure something out," Sara screamed back to me.

While Sara thought, I prayed: *Lord, thank You for keeping us safe. I know You're still with us.*

We dropped another three feet. The carnival had disappeared from sight. It looked like gremlins and skeletons were racing next to our car. This ride was too weird, way too weird.

Then it suddenly slowed down and started to rise toward the surface again. Once we were back at the top, the car stopped and the safety bar opened. I breathed a sigh of relief.

The Tilt-a-Whirl had barely stopped before we hit the ground. I had only taken two steps when I heard something crack. I looked up to see the *A* from the sign come loose. It fell with a thud into the car we had been riding in. I ran after the others.

Sammy had turned down an alley of the midway. "I think the gate out is this way," he said.

As we followed him, I told the others about the *A* that had fallen from the sign. Brent put it together. He said, "*It's only a*—but what is it only?"

Sammy jammed his high-tops into the dirt so quickly that we almost ran into him.

I saw why he stopped so suddenly.

There before us was a stage. On the stage was a ventriloquist with his dummy. The dummy was dressed in a plaid shirt and bib overalls. The ventriloquist wore a dark suit and a red bow tie.

We stared at them.

"Hello, kids," the dummy said. "It's time for another

terrible show—knot. Get it? Knot." He chuckled and pointed to the ventriloquist's bow tie.

"Hey, kids. I went to the doctor the other day because I thought I caught the flu bug. He said, 'Here's something for the bug,' and he gave me a woodpecker. Get it? Woodpecker. Ha, ha, ha. I've got a million of them."

Sammy laughed right along with him. I shifted from foot to foot. This whole place made me feel tense. Nothing here was what it was supposed to be.

Nothing turned out the way it should.

Nothing made sense.

I knew I wasn't looking at it from the right perspective, but I wasn't sure what the right perspective was. If this were a dream or something in a book, all this stuff would be understandable, even funny.

But this wasn't a book. It wasn't TV. It wasn't a dream. I, Kyle Conlon, was living through a real, live, crazy adventure. And why? What was I supposed to be learning? That "God's spirit, who is in you, is greater than the devil, who is in the world"? That God can be trusted in every situation? That the Lord watches over us at all times?

Sara snapped me from my thoughts when she asked the dummy a question. "Would you tell us some more jokes?"

"Wood I? Get it? Wood eye," the dummy answered,

pointing to his eyeball. "Ha, ha, ha. I got a million of them."

The ventriloquist looked at us and smiled. His teeth were white and perfectly straight. His blue eyes had a blank look, as if there was little behind them.

"I've got a better idea. Instead of more jokes, how about a nice trick or two? I will need a volunteer from the audience."

Sara leaped to the stage. "I'm ready. What do I need to do?"

"Come closer, my friend," said the dummy.

What was Sara trying to prove? I had a bad feeling about this, and it was confirmed when the dummy leaped off the ventriloquist's lap and onto Sara. The force of the dummy hitting her knocked Sara to the stage.

It didn't look like the ventriloquist threw him. I was almost sure the dummy had jumped on his own.

But dummies don't do anything on their own. The ventriloquist does all the moving.

The dummy's wooden hands and fingers grabbed at Sara, frightening her. She screamed for help.

I cupped my hands around my mouth and yelled to the ventriloquist. He just sat there.

I leaped onto the stage and raced up to him. I pushed his arm to get his attention, but the ventriloquist slumped into the chair.

Then he slid off, making a heavy wooden thud on

the stage. He was lifeless, and I saw the joints in his jawbone. They were hinged together by bolts.

He was the dummy.

Whatever had grabbed Sara was not a dummy. It was alive, and Sara needed help.

Sammy saw what happened with the ventriloquist and jumped onto the stage. He was thinking like I was. We both dived for the mysterious fiend at the same time and smacked our heads hard against each other.

I tumbled off the back of the stage. Sammy rolled off the front. Sara screamed again.

Brent moved so quickly that by the time I was able to pull my aching head and body onto the stage again, he was reaching for the impostor dummy. The moment his hands grabbed the menace, it went limp. We stared at the body, now lying lifeless on the stage. It, too, was made of wood.

"Thanks, Brent. I was beginning to think that you three were drawing straws to see who had to help me," Sara said as she took in some deep breaths to calm herself.

"I don't get it," Brent said. "This was a dummy too. How could it have acted so lifelike?"

"I don't know," I said. "But I don't think I want to hang around here and find out."

Sammy seemed unfazed by the experience, as though he had just witnessed nothing more than a magic trick. "So what's next?" he asked.

"Nothing!" Brent and I said simultaneously. We had had enough of this mania and wanted to leave.

Sammy stomped his feet in a mock temper tantrum. "I don't want to go. I don't want to go."

Sara added, "I don't think we should stay any longer. Let's just get out of here. I think the gate is this way." She started walking, and we all followed along.

"Okay," Sammy said, "but if we leave now we'll never solve the mystery of Dr. Shivers' Carnival of Terror."

Brent added his two cents' worth. "I don't care. I'm out of here."

"There is something really strange going on around here," Sara said. "I wish we could figure it out. But frankly, I'm too spooked to stay."

"The sign said THE MAGIC DUMMY. Do you think it's magic?" I asked. I don't believe in such things but this place was so weird.

"Magic is just a bunch of tricks that magicians learn. It's not real. But I wonder what's really going on here," Sara answered with a puzzled look on her face.

Sammy wanted to make sure that we knew where he stood. "I love this place. I'm thinking of coming back tomorrow when it opens up. I feel like I've missed some of the best stuff. Besides, I've got to get one of those barking hot dogs to take back home with us. I've got to scare my little brother with it."

"What a guy. I don't ever want to see this place again. Tomorrow is too soon. Next week is too soon. Next month is too soon. Next—"

I stopped Brent in the middle of his sentence. I heard something.

We were only thirty feet from the gate when I heard footsteps, lots of footsteps heading our way. We spun around and saw a large crowd of people stampeding toward us. I saw several clowns in the crowd.

They must have known we were getting ready to leave. Dr. Shivers' gang was going to make sure that we didn't.

As they got closer, the four of us jumped out of the way. They didn't even slow down. They ran right by us.

Why would they race as fast as they could our way and then not grab us? It didn't make sense.

Then I saw the reason. A large, roaring lion bounded around the corner. His hungry eyes looked directly at us.

I looked around. Our only escape was to enter the closest amusement. It was only three feet away. The lion was about twenty feet away.

I had no choice. I grabbed Brent and Sammy by the arms and yelled to Sara. In two seconds we were falling backward through the door of a place called THE MUMMY'S TOMB. It had an unusual sign. Most of the letters were big, squared shapes. But one of the *M*s was exactly like the cursive *M* in the magic dummy sign. Could that be our next clue?

Inside the scene looked like the set of an Egyptian movie. Fake sandstone blocks were stacked along the walls. Flat human forms with their arms bent funny were painted on the blocks. It didn't look very scary.

Sara looked around at the paintings. "Hey, this could be really educational. I've been doing research on ancient Egypt for a report, so I can say that I did research on my Christmas vacation."

"Yeah, research on how to get scared to death," Brent tossed in.

"What I'm scared of right now is that lion outside. At least we're safe from it in here. Besides, maybe I can learn something," Sara said.

"About all you're going to learn is how to make a cheesy movie set. Let's just leave," I said.

"If you want to be eaten by a lion, go ahead. I'm staying in here a while," she answered.

Sara had a point. Our options were to stay inside the Mummy's Tomb or leave and risk becoming lunch for a hungry lion.

"You're right," I said. "We're safer in here than out there. I don't see anything in here that looks threatening."

We descended a staircase. Behind large panes of glass we saw wax mummies authentically positioned in their tombs. Interesting historical facts were printed on metal plaques next to each window.

Sammy was bored. "Hey, let's hurry it along here."

We descended more stairs and passed more and more windows. After about forty steps I stopped everyone. "Have any of you noticed the same thing I noticed?"

Brent was the first to answer. "Yeah, why are we going downstairs? How could we go any deeper? This carnival was put up just last night while we slept. Nobody would have had time to dig out a hole this deep. Now I've got the shivers."

"This whole place gives me the shivers," I added.

Sammy chimed in, "Yeah, Dr. Shivers."

"Let's turn around and get out of here," Brent said. "I don't think there's anything else worth seeing. That lion's got to be gone by now."

"I'm with Brent," I said. With that, I turned to walk back up the stairs.

I froze.

My voice caught in my throat and my mouth went dry.

Only three steps away from me was a figure wrapped in cloth strips. It was a mummy.

My friends twisted their heads quickly and saw the mummy standing behind me.

My mouth was wide open. After everything we had seen, I should have been ready for another fright. I wasn't. No one else was either.

We had been looking at all the glass-encased wax mummies and didn't expect that a real one would suddenly appear behind us.

I was still trying to form words when Brent screamed, "Run, everybody, run!"

Holding on to the rail for balance, we took three steps at a time down the staircase. How many more steps we took I don't know. I was too frightened to count, and the mummy was bounding down behind us. Its wrappings kept it from moving too fast, and that may have saved us.

The monster yelled, "You have violated my tomb. I am coming for you."

His eerie, deep rough voice was enough to keep us running.

Sammy stumbled when he hit bottom. He fell against the wall and slipped to the floor.

Sara leaped over him to keep from tripping, but Brent wasn't so lucky. He went sprawling along the ground as well. I was able to stop myself in front of them.

"Quick, get up. We don't have time for a rest," I yelled.

"Who's resting?" Brent answered. "Sammy fell, and I tripped over him. Help us up."

"You have violated my tomb." The voice was closer as it called to us.

"This way!" Sara yelled. "I've found another room."

Sammy scrambled to his feet as I pulled Brent to his. "We've got to find a way out of here. I don't think this guy likes houseguests," I said to the others.

Even Sammy seemed nervous now. He shot back, "Another brilliant deduction, Sherlock. I really don't need you to give me a running commentary of what is going on. I just want to get out of here."

We raced behind Sara into the big room. All around us we saw gold jewelry and statues with human bodies and animal heads. It was really strange.

"Great," Sammy snapped at Sara. "Now we're trapped in some room with no way out. We've got an angry mummy that doesn't plan on just grounding us but putting us into the ground and there isn't a way out. Can this get any worse?"

"You have violated my tomb. I am coming for you." The mummy sounded very close.

"I think it just got worse. He's right outside," Sara said.

I yelled instructions to everyone. "Quick, grab some of those statues and push them in front of the door. It will keep him out for a few minutes. Brent, start looking for a way out of here."

Brent panicked. "Like what, Kyle?"

"A button, a switch. Anything that might move a wall. All of Dr. Shivers' amusements have had a trick to get out. Look for the one here."

Brent felt along the walls while the rest of us pushed statues across the door. After the third one, I felt we might keep the mummy out long enough to find an escape.

"You cannot stop me. I am coming for you. You have violated my tomb," he called to us in his low, raspy voice.

I didn't want to stick around to find out whether he meant it or not. I began pushing on the walls. I thought that there might be a fake wall or a hidden door.

Brent pulled everything in sight to see if some object would open up a sliding door to another passageway.

Sammy and Sara piled more Egyptian artifacts in front of the door to keep the mummy out.

The mummy continued to call to us, "You have violated my tomb. I am coming for you."

Sammy ran toward me. As he neared me, his foot caught in an Egyptian necklace and he tripped. His body soared through the air then hit a casket. As he fell back away from it, the door to the casket popped open. A dim light shone from somewhere deep within the casket.

Brent turned and yelled, "Sammy, what did you do?"

I didn't have time to see the damage caused by his fall. Our mummy friend pushed through the statues in front of the doorway and was stepping over them.

Soon he would have us in his grasp.

"We're doomed!" I yelled.

Sara jumped out of the mummy's way and headed right toward us, then she made a quick cut and ran for the open casket. "Follow me and don't ask questions," she called as she raced by.

Sammy and Brent bumped into each other as they dived through the casket door. I turned to see where the mummy was. My delay cost me big time. His large, wrapped hands grabbed me by the shoulders. I was only inches from the casket.

Four hands reached from inside the casket and grabbed me. *Oh, no,* I thought. *I'm part of a mummy tug-of-war.* I could see the newspaper headline now: BOY TORN APART BY MUMMIES. I was scared.

The four hands inside the casket won the battle, pulling me hard into another room. I was moving so fast that I fell and landed facedown onto the dirty floor. Rolling over, I opened my eyes.

It couldn't be.

I was lying between Sammy and Sara on the dusty

floor of another room in the tomb. "Thanks. That one was really close. I wasn't sure if I was ever going to get out of the mummy's hands. Do you have any idea where we are?"

"I haven't had time to look around, but this looks like the room where they prepared the mummies for burial. If I'm right, there will be a secret door here that leads to the outside. The people who prepared the mummies had to confuse grave robbers so the treasure would be safe," Sara explained.

"Let's get going. I want out of here as quickly as possible," Brent added.

Each of us searched the room for the secret door. Sammy climbed the rocks that jutted out from the wall to search the ceiling, while Sara searched the floor. Brent felt along the stone wall.

"Nothing. There is nothing here," Sara said with frustration in her voice.

"Keep looking, Sara. We have to find a way out. Besides, that mummy knows all the ways into this place. I wouldn't be surprised if he mysteriously showed up out of the shadows. So keep looking," Brent insisted.

She went back to feeling and tugging on each rock. Brent pushed every painted symbol on the wall. There wasn't much light inside our mummy preparation room.

A torch on the wall gave us enough light to see,

but that most likely would not last as long as we needed it.

Sara stood up and straightened her spine. "I'm getting sore bending over. I wish we were back at your uncle's house relaxing in the hot tub, Kyle."

"I want to swim in the pool and get some of this dirt off me," Sammy called down from his search of the high points of the wall.

"Now you're making sense, Sammy. I hope this means you don't want to go on any more rides," I said.

"Yeah," Brent said. "There may not be anything like this back in our little town, but I, for one, am mighty glad."

The torchlight was getting dimmer. I needed to do something to stretch our lighting. While the others looked for the passage, I went through the bottles of fluids and stone boxes.

If I could find a liquid that burned, I would dip some old cloth strips in it and wrap them around a torch. I saw that in a movie once.

It worked for the hero on the big screen. I hoped it would work for me as well.

There was one large vial on the top shelf over a stone table. I grabbed it, but I couldn't lift it off the shelf. Instead, it fell forward as if it were hinged.

I stood on tiptoe to get a better look, when all of a sudden a horrible grinding noise made me spin around.

"What's that noise? What's happening?" I hurriedly asked the others.

"That large stone over there is moving," Brent answered fearfully.

We all watched as a square piece of stone about the size of a refrigerator began to slide forward. As it inched toward us, I felt the hairs rise on the back of my neck and chills run up and down my spine. What could this be? What would come out of there?

A hand curled around the stone. It was wrapped heavily in cloth strips. I was sure that our mummy was coming again.

Sara jumped back and bumped into Brent, who was already retreating. When her body struck Brent's, he stumbled over some stones on the floor and lost his balance. Brent hit the ground hard. I heard the thud and raced toward him.

Sammy leaped away from the wall and grabbed a wooden beam. From there he swung like a monkey to a torch holder. When he grabbed the torch holder it gave way and flipped downward.

By accident, Sammy had found the hidden lever that opened the secret passage to the outside.

Unfortunately, the mummy was already slipping in the other passageway and three of us were lying on the floor.

I yanked hard on Brent's arm and pulled him to his feet. Sara was already scrambling up, and Sammy's tumble to the ground lasted only a second.

We had to get out of there before the mummy reached us. I didn't know what this mummy wanted to do to us, but I was certain he didn't intend to give us a loving hug.

Brent was still groggy from his fall. I guided him toward the passageway and pushed his body through. He stumbled again and fell. Inside the opening was another staircase.

Sara and I hoisted Brent up. Sara supported Brent under one of his arms and I took the other. We began to drag him up the steps.

Sammy was left with the unfortunate job of holding the mummy back until we climbed the stairs. I don't know what he did, but whatever it was, it worked.

The three of us had reached the top when I heard Sammy's shoes slapping the stone stairway. He was only a few inches behind us as we turned the corner and discovered ourselves at a fork in the staircase.

The mummy was halfway up the steps. We heard him shouting his favorite and only phrase, "You have violated my tomb. I am coming for you."

"Which way do we go?" I asked the others.

Sara thought a moment and said, "Left."

Sammy said, "Right."

"We only have a few more seconds to make the decision here. Which way?" I pressed for one unified answer.

Brent stood on his own now and studied the stairways. "Definitely left," he said.

"That's good enough for me." I reached to help Brent up the steps, but it was obvious he no longer needed help. The four of us ran up the stairs.

I was near the top of the staircase when I looked behind me to see where my friends were. I should have been looking ahead, because as I hit the top landing my body crunched into another one.

I looked up. It was the mummy. His big hands locked me in a tight hold. He said over and over again, "You have violated my tomb. I am coming for you." Only he didn't have to come for me. He already had me.

"Don't come the rest of the way up the stairs!" I yelled, panic straining my voice. My friends stopped below me.

"What do we do?" Sammy asked.

Sara didn't wait to find out what the others were going to say. She ran as fast as she could back down the steps.

The mummy dragged me along the hallway. I twisted from side to side, trying to break free, but the mummy was too strong. He picked me up and slung me over his shoulder.

I could hear Brent panicking. "It's my fault! I chose this staircase. Kyle's caught and it's my fault!"

The mummy turned a bend in the corridor, then halted. I didn't know if that was a good or bad sign. I twisted around to see what made him stop.

Sara stood in front of us with a flaming torch. "All

right, mummy. There is nothing that this blazing, fiery torch would like more than to set fire to a bunch of old rags wrapped around some two-thousand-year-old withered body. So, drop my friend and you go free."

The move was extremely bold. And it worked. The mummy hurried away to some other part of his Egyptian tomb. Sara had saved me. "Hurry!" she said, not waiting for me to thank her. "Let's get back to the staircase."

"Thanks," I said as I started running. "That was a brave thing you did. What made you think of it?"

"I didn't know what else to do but pray," Sara said with a twinkle in her eye. "And God gave me the courage to stand up to that mummy!"

Sara and I ran back down the hall and found Brent and Sammy seemingly frozen on the steps, their eyes opened wide in fear. When Brent saw me he let out a wail, "Kyle. Oh, Kyle, I thought you were—"

"Come on," I interrupted. "No time for that now. Let's get moving."

We raced to the bottom of the steps and got to the other staircase. We climbed it to the top. We walked another few steps and came to a dead end in the stone-lined hallway. There was no way out.

"I can't figure this out," I said. "One of these stairways should have led us out of here." I turned to tell the others that we needed to go back.

There was no one behind me. My friends had vanished.

"Sara! Sammy! Brent!" I called their names, but no answer came back to me. They'd been right behind me only a moment before.

I imagined that the mummy had grabbed them. I needed to save them, but how? Feeling helpless and hopeless, I slumped down in the corner.

For the first time that day I felt like crying. I wanted out of this mummy's tomb and out of the carnival.

I heaved a breath. *Lord,* I prayed, *if I were all by myself, I'd be no match for a mummy. But I've got You with me. I know I'll be all right.*

I stood up and started back down the dark passageway. I moved slowly and quietly until I heard voices. I stopped.

My heart beat so loudly that I couldn't hear what was being said. I knew I needed to go closer, but I was too scared. For several moments I stood silently, leaning against the stone wall.

Then I pulled together all the courage I had and made a step toward the voices. They were barely audible, but I recognized them—Sammy, Sara, and Brent.

"Hey guys! I'm here! It's me!" I shouted, but they didn't hear me.

I could hear Sammy say, "The mummy must have grabbed Kyle. He was up ahead of us and then he was gone. I think we need to go back and look for him."

"How are we going to look for him? We don't have a torch since Sara's burned out. We don't have a flashlight. We don't have any idea where he might be," Brent said.

"That doesn't make any difference to me. Kyle is lost and we need to find him," Sara objected. "Besides, we've hit a dead end. This passage leads nowhere."

They were in the same predicament that I was in. I went down another corridor that led to nowhere and so did they. If the ones we chose did not lead to safety then there must not be a way out. Or there must be another passage we missed as we traveled along the stone hallway.

"Let's go find him," Sara said. I could hear her footsteps coming toward me. The others were right behind her. Their steps sounded so close to me. "Hey, you guys! I'm here! This way!"

I waited, but their steps never got any closer. In fact, they now headed away from me. They must have found the passageway out. I had to catch up to them.

I started down the corridor, feeling my way along the rocks. I moved slowly, touching from side to side. I knew that if I could feel the opening I would find my friends. It was my only hope.

After a few minutes, I thought that I should have found the passage opening. I started to get frightened.

I felt from one side to the other as I prayed.

My right hand touched stone. My left hand touched stone.

My right hand touched stone. My left hand touched rags.

I pulled it away quickly. What was that? I heard deep, heavy breathing, then a growling whisper that moved closer and closer to my ear.

"You have violated my tomb. I am coming for you."

"Aah!" I shrieked. I backed away from the mummy. When I did that I felt no stone behind me. The passageway was right there.

The monster's hand reached out and grabbed me, but it didn't get a good hold on me. I broke free and went hurtling down the open corridor behind me.

The mummy's cloth-wrapped feet thudded along the stones. It was too close for me to feel safe.

"Help! Sammy, Sara, Brent, where are you? The mummy is right behind me. We need to get out of here and we need to do it right now."

"Kyle, run toward my voice," Sara yelled.

She was close, but I suddenly realized how stupid I was. I had just led the mummy right to my friends. We had not found the way out yet. The mummy was inches away from me.

In the dark, I couldn't tell how close I was to them. I found out soon enough; I slammed into them and we all went flying into the stones at the end of the hallway.

When we hit the wall I felt it move slightly and then pop open. The sunlight bathed us as we tumbled to the dirt midway of Dr. Shivers' Carnival of Terror. We had to shut our eyes to protect them from the brightness.

Brent let out a long breath. Sara gasped. I was confused. Sammy had a very different response from the rest of us and a very typical one for him. He was giggling.

"That was great," Sammy said. "I like this place more and more."

"Maybe you like it so much because you weren't grabbed by a mummy," I snapped back at him as I stood dusting myself off.

"Or because you didn't eat any worm-filled cotton candy," Brent added.

"And you didn't get attacked by a living dummy," Sara threw in for good measure. "I vote that we get out of here. I don't even care about the mystery any more." Sara moved into the center of our group and looked each of us in the eyes. I was with her all the way until I took a step back onto something slippery. I lost my balance and went crashing to the ground once again.

"What's the matter? Are you so worn out that you need a nap before we leave?" Sammy kidded.

"No, I slipped on something," I snapped back.

"You slipped on our clue." Sara said, suddenly interested in the mystery again as she pointed downward. "There's an *O* painted on the ground. The plot thickens, my friends. If we add that to the *M* from the mummy's tomb sign, we know that *It's only a mo* . . . But what is a mo?"

We all tried to finish the phrase.

"It's only a mouse."

"It's only a mockingbird."

"Mocha candy."

"Monkey."

"Mongoose."

"Monster."

When Brent said *monster*, we all mouthed the phrase together. "It's only a monster." Shivers ran up and down my spine.

Then Sammy piped up again. "So it's only a monster. I still want a prize before we go. There's a ball toss over there. Let me do that and then we can get out of here quickly." Sammy ran toward the game booth before any of us had time to respond.

A barker appeared as we approached the game. He had a big, beaming smile. Glancing at our necklaces, he said, "Ah, you are friends of Dr. Shivers. What can I do for you? Do you want to win a prize?"

"That's what we're here for. What do we have to do, sir?" Sammy asked.

"Simple, my friends. Just knock over the bottles in three tries," the barker answered.

Sammy picked up the balls, but then paused. He looked at Sara. "You're the best pitcher here. Why don't you try? If you win me a prize, I'll gladly leave."

"All right," Sara agreed. "Anything to get out of here quickly."

Sara tossed the first ball. It hit the bottles and the top one fell off. The next time she hit the center one and they all fell but one. On her third attempt the last bottle fell.

"You won," Brent shouted, "but where did the guy go?"

"Right here, I just had to get the prize."

His back was to us. When he turned around, his beaming smile had turned into bloodstained fangs. His face was covered with dripping green skin, and his eyes glowed bright red.

"Aah!" we yelled in unison.

The barker laughed and gripped his face with his hands. He pulled off a mask. He was now howling with laughter. "That gets them every time. I love doing that to kids."

Sammy grabbed the mask right away, but Brent took it from his hands.

Brent put it on and tried to scare us all with it. After what we had been through a little mask didn't seem to have much effect.

I looked at the barker while Brent tried to scare Sara. He raised his hand and gave me a victory sign.

Then Brent handed the mask to Sammy, and he slipped it over his head. He goofed off a little with it then tried to remove it.

"Hey, I can't get it off," Sammy cried out.

"Quit messing around, Samuel," Brent said very seriously.

"I agree," I said with emphasis.

"Help me. It feels like it's sticking to my skin. It's starting to feel *like* my skin. Quick, help me," Sammy whimpered.

His body started to twist away from us. I thought he was in pain. Suddenly he stood straight up with his back to us.

I felt relieved that he seemed to be back to himself. Sammy turned very slowly. His arms were raised in the air. His eyes were red and horrible looking. He spoke to us, "Dr. Shivers has sent me to eliminate all of you. I must do as the good doctor says."

The mask had been loose when Sammy first put it on. Now it was drawn tightly over his face and neck.

He took a step toward us. We huddled together. I don't know what the others were thinking, but I was torn. *Do I help my friend or do I run for my life?*

I turned to the other two. "Sara, you and I will hold Sammy down while Brent pulls off the mask." They nodded in agreement.

We lunged at Sammy. Sara and I held Sammy on the ground while Brent pounced on Sammy's chest. Brent grabbed for the mask and I heard Sammy laugh.

"Got you, didn't I?" he said.

It was the first time I ever saw Brent want to hit anybody. He formed a fist with his right hand and grimaced, but he held back.

"I guess I shouldn't have done that. I'm sorry, everyone. I thought it would be funny. I guess I'm ready to leave if you are. Which way is out?"

"I kind of remember that the front gate was over by that balloon stand. We can all get one of those really scary balloons and head back to Kyle's uncle's," Brent said.

"To the balloons!" Sara yelled, and I raced toward the booth. I stopped dead in my tracks in front of it. The balloons were there, but the vendor wasn't.

A moment before, a woman dressed in a bright red jacket had been standing next to the balloons smiling at us. Now she was gone.

Sara ran up behind me. She laughed and said, "I'm second."

Then she gasped. "Where is the woman who was here a minute ago?"

"That's what I was just wondering. I saw her, and I don't remember taking my eyes off the balloons. How could she have slipped away so quickly? Let's just skip the balloons and get out of this place," I told her.

Brent was with us next. "I really want to get a balloon," he said.

"All right. But after this I'm going home," I told him firmly.

"We all keep saying that and then something else happens. This is not an easy place to get out of," Sara added.

The three of us started pulling at the balloon strings. Sara chose one that had Dracula painted on it. Hers came out easily.

Brent's was a little tougher. He tugged and tugged on the string of a face that looked more like a monster than most monster masks in stores. It finally came loose, and he stood waiting for me.

My choice was a little less frightening. It was a cute little animal face. The problem was that my string wouldn't come loose at all. The three of us grabbed the string and yanked it. It wouldn't budge.

"I surrender. I'll take something else."

The moment I said that, the balloon popped loose and started floating in the air. We all jumped for it, but the helium was lighter than we were and the balloon continued to rise.

"This just isn't my day. I can't even pick a balloon without something strange happening. I'll choose another one."

I walked back toward the balloons, but my eyes were still focused on the one I lost.

Bang!

"Somebody is shooting at us!" Brent said. "Hit the dirt!"

We were on the ground in a second.

"Who is shooting at us?" Sara asked. She was quiet for a minute and then cried out, "Where's Sammy? Where did he go? Have either one of you two seen him?"

I sat up and stared around, but I didn't see Sammy. I yelled for him, "Sammy, where are you? Quit goofing around, Sammy. Come on, don't joke around like this."

No answer. I climbed to my feet just as another shot rang out.

Bang!

Before I could hit the ground again, balloon fragments fell on my head. I shook them off and looked up.

I saw a piece of paper floating to the ground. It must have been inside the balloon. The shot must have been to break the balloon.

"What is it?" Brent asked.

I picked up the paper. "It's a message to us. I think it has something to do with Sammy."

Sara grabbed the paper out of my hand.

"What does it say, Sara?" Brent asked.

"'We have something that you may want back. Come to the Tunnel of the Weird.'"

"What do you think it means?" I asked.

"I think you were right. I think someone has kidnapped Sammy and we have to get him back. He's probably at this Tunnel of the Weird," Sara said.

"Where is it?" I asked. "Everything in this place is weird. I think we need to have that old-fashioned prayer meeting. Let's pray for Sammy's protection." We formed a circle, held hands, and prayed for a few minutes. There was real power in our prayer, and we all could feel it.

"Now, let's find that tunnel," Sara said with a new strength in her voice.

"I haven't seen anything like that anywhere in the carnival," Brent said.

"We better split up and look for it. I don't think we have much time. We need to find him now," Sara said firmly.

"I think we should ask someone where it is," Brent said.

"Where are we going to find someone to ask?" I snapped.

Brent looked around, his eyes growing wider and wider. "Over there," he said.

Sara and I turned around quickly on our heels.

It was the clown.

The clown lifted his arm and waved. He motioned to us to follow him. Then he started to walk down another midway of rides and games, ones that we had not seen before. I couldn't believe how big the carnival was. How could they have built this overnight?

The clown stayed about ten feet ahead of us. I didn't mind that. He was a strange character to say the least.

He passed a lemonade stand and turned right, disappearing from our sight. By the time we got around the corner, he was gone. I wasn't sure where to look for him.

There were several rides and other amusements that he could have slipped into. But it didn't make any difference where he had gone. We were looking for the Tunnel of the Weird.

"I see it over there," Sara said, pointing straight ahead. The sign over the entrance looked old, and it hung by one rusty nail from one side. The wind was making it swing back and forth. We heard it squeak.

"Do you hear that?" I asked.

"What?" Sara said.

"I can hear the sign squeaking."

Sara looked at me like I was crazy.

"The music from the public address system has been turned off. I'm beginning to think that this Tunnel of the Weird is not a safe place for any of us," I said fearfully.

Brent put his hand on my shoulder, then stepped toward the tunnel. "We don't have a choice. Sammy has been kidnapped and we need to find him."

"I'm all for it, but I think we should have some sort of game plan," Sara added.

"I've got one. Let's go in and get Sammy and get back out alive," Brent said matter-of-factly. "We don't know what's in there. We need to stay close together and grab Sammy as soon as we can.

"I'll guide us in. Sara, you guide us out. Kyle will take the lead against any monster that we might find in there. Agreed?"

"I'm ready," Sara said.

"Me too," I chirped.

We walked the few feet toward the tunnel with slow, fearful steps. The entrance was a heavy, dark brown wooden door. We slowly pushed our way through it.

Inside, it was very dark. I could hear an amusement ride car on a track near me.

"I'll go first," Brent said as he moved by me. "Can you see the cars for the ride?"

"Over here, children."

The voice came out of the dim light. My eyes had adjusted to the low lights by now. A soft glow lit the face of a man on the other side of the tracks.

He continued, "Welcome to the Tunnel of the Weird. Many go in. Few come out. Would you have a seat please?"

The bar to the car popped up and the three of us climbed in. I looked at the man and asked, "What do you mean by 'few come out'?" He didn't answer. In another moment the car lurched forward. I turned back to look at the man, but he was gone. We were entering the tunnel.

Brent relaxed. "I've seen this ride before. They have it at the Big America Theme Park."

"What happens?" Sara quizzed.

"I don't know for sure. I mean, I've never ridden the one at Big America. I've only seen it. I've heard that a bunch of things jump out and try to scare you. None of it is real. Relax and enjoy the ride," he said. Sara and I wanted to believe him.

The first thing we saw was a headless woman sitting in a rocking chair. Her head was in her lap and it was talking to us. "Turn back now. Go no farther, or you may never come out of here again."

"I think we should believe her and leave," I said.

"You want to leave Sammy?" Brent asked.

"No. You're right, we have to find him. But I hope we can do it fast," I answered, just as the headless woman receded into the darkness.

The car turned a corner and came alongside a lumberjack dressed in a red plaid shirt, stocking cap, and jeans. He flashed a giant smile and raised his ax.

"I don't like the looks of this," I said.

Brent tried to assure me. "Haven't you ever seen one of those before? It's a robot. He'll lower the ax in a minute."

And he did.

He started to lower it quickly and let go of it. The handle and glistening ax head flew our way. We dived for the floor of the amusement car. I heard the ax smash into the front of the car with a loud bang.

I was afraid to look, but I raised my head just slightly and peeked outside the car.

The lumberjack was gone. I looked at the front of the amusement car, and the ax was gone too. There was no sign of either one anywhere.

"It's all right. The lumberjack is gone and his ax never really hit us," I said, exhaling a sigh of relief.

Sara popped up and looked at me. "What happened?" she asked.

Before I could reply, Brent spoke up. "It was weird, and we are in the Tunnel of the Weird."

Sara's mouth fell open and she spit out the words, "Weirdness ahead!"

Brent and I turned to see our car heading directly for a spinning buzz saw. "Jump out of the car," I screamed.

"That's crazy. There's nothing but wall on both sides of us. We're about to become split personalities!" Sara said, panic rising in her voice.

In another minute we would be doing more than panicking. In another minute we would be going to pieces—literally.

"Move to the sides of the car and let the blade pass down the middle," I yelled to the others.

Sara and Brent moved to the left side of the car and I went for the right.

The car moved closer and closer to the blade. The sound got louder.

We were about a foot from the blade. I could feel the breeze from the fast-turning toothed wheel. I prayed that we would survive the cut.

Then we were about six inches away. Suddenly the car shifted and my body faced the blade.

I gulped.

"Help!" I screamed. As I did that the car leaped forward, pulling us out of the way of the whirling blade.

"That was close," Sara cried.

"Too close," I agreed.

Brent sat back and spoke. "We came in here to save Sammy, and it looks like we may not make it out of here."

"Yes, we will," I said, trying to banish Brent's fears, although I wasn't convinced myself that we would make it out of the Tunnel of the Weird. "The Lord will show us where Sammy is and help us get out of this place."

"Then let's get to work and find him because I want to get out of here as quickly as possible," Sara added.

Her statement was almost drowned out by the sound of rushing water. We looked at each other and then at what was ahead of us.

Our car had gone into a flowing stream of water

that ran through the tunnel. And that stream headed straight for a waterfall. We couldn't tell how far down it was, but the crashing water sounds at the bottom were loud and violent.

"Hang on!" Sara yelled to make sure her voice sounded out above the water.

We all gripped the bar in front of us. I looked over at Brent. His eyes were closed and his lips were moving. I think he was praying. Sara was praying out loud.

We hit the edge and tipped forward.

Down and down the car fell.

The air rushed by us faster and faster.

We anticipated the crash, but it seemed like it was never going to come.

"I don't think we're going to come out of this one. I'm really sorry for inviting you out here to my uncle's house. I wanted us to have fun, but it seems like the fun ends right here," I apologized as we dropped through the rushing water.

Brent opened his mouth to say something when the car blasted into a pool of water and came to a dead stop, tossing us forward against the crash bar. It saved us from flying out and into the water. None of us were hurt.

"Wow! That was fantastic," Sara exclaimed. "I wonder what we're in for next?"

I looked at Brent. His face was greenish. "I'm not

feeling too good," he said. "All this excitement is making my stomach tie in knots."

Sara didn't hear what he said. Her eyes were fixed on something in front of us—a castle. Its turrets were built from large stones.

I wondered again how the carnival workers built all this in one night. I needed to remember to ask Dr. Shivers when we got out of here. *If* we got out of here.

Our little car was moving again, heading straight for the big wooden door. It was a drawbridge, but it had not been let down yet. After the other weird things we had encountered in this tunnel I fully expected it to lower and take us inside. I was right.

The drawbridge eased down as we got closer. By the time our car got to the moat, the bridge was all the way down. We crossed it. Not one of us said a word. Our silence told me that each of us was frightened about what we would encounter next. We entered the castle. It was so dark inside that we could not see a thing. I heard the drawbridge rise again and close tightly behind us. We were not going to go back that way. We had no choice but to press ahead. Then the amusement car stopped. Sara sucked in a breath. Brent let out his breath, and I felt thankful to still have mine running through my lungs.

"What's next?" Brent asked.

"We have to stay calm."

We heard the sound of several feet stomping toward us in the dark. It sounded like people wearing some type of armor.

The clanking metal grew louder, and we knew our welcoming committee was almost on us.

Sara yelled, "Run for it!" I felt her body leap from the car and then I heard a crash against metal. "Let me go!" Sara yelled.

"Sara, are you all right?" Brent called out into the darkness. I felt hands brush by me, and Brent yelped and began to struggle. Then two strong hands grabbed me under my arms and another pair took hold of my legs.

We had been captured, but by what?

"Where are you taking us?" I demanded. No answer, only the sound of our captors' grunts.

Sara's voice and Brent's were not too far from me. The captors carried us off in the dark. I had no idea where we were going, and I was afraid of where it could be.

Even though it was too dark to see, I could sense that we were placed inside a room. Brent breathed heavily and Sara whispered a prayer. But I was sure that there was another person in the room with us.

"Who's there?" I asked.

"Me," a voice replied.

"Sammy!" we yelled in unison.

"Man, am I glad to see you," I said. "That is if we could really see you. How did you get in here?"

"I'm not sure. When the three of you went to get balloons, I saw one of those hot dog stands and I wanted to get a barking hot dog for my little brother. When I got closer to the hot dog stand, one of the carnival workers invited me to try a new ride called the Well of Doom.

"I guess I'm a real sucker. I sat down in a bucket, and suddenly a dozen crazy things happened to me. To make a really weird story short, I ended up here," he told us.

"That's pretty close to how we got here. Now we need to find a way out of here. Any ideas?" Sara asked.

"Have you found the walls or a door yet?" I asked.

"No, I just got here a few seconds before you did. It's too dark to see anything," he answered.

"I have an idea," Brent said with excitement.

"Spit it out," Sara said. "Anything would be helpful right now."

"We need to find a wall, but we don't know where the closest one is. I have a way to find it," he said. "I have some of that glow-in-the-dark putty that comes in an egg in my pocket.

"We can roll it into a ball that we can throw against the walls. When it hits, it will bounce back. Then we head to the closest wall," he told us with pride.

"That is the best idea I've heard in the last five minutes. I say we go for it," I encouraged.

The next thing I knew Brent was throwing the putty ball in the four directions around us. The first one took a while to come back. The second and third throws returned faster. The fourth one told us that we were only about three feet from a wall.

Sara got to the wall first and pushed on it. Brent felt around for an opening. Sammy got frustrated and kicked the wall.

I was about to tell him not to lose his temper when the wall gave a cracking sound. He kicked again. Something popped open.

"It's the door!" Brent yelled happily.

"Pure luck," Sara told Sammy.

"What do you mean? I knew exactly what I was doing," he joked.

"I think we should get out of here before something else happens," I warned them.

We passed through the doorway and stopped. We had stepped into what looked like a beautiful field. Bright lights shone above us, and what looked like green plastic grass covered the ground.

I looked behind us. The door we came through was in the side of a wall. The number sixteen was painted on it.

"Where are we?" Brent asked with bewilderment.

"It looks like a big, green field," I told him as I

walked forward and looked around for a clue. "It doesn't look familiar, but we must be outside the carnival. Let's find our way back to my uncle's."

I raised my foot to take another step, but something grabbed me by the belt and hurled me to the ground.

"Why did you do that, Sammy?" I lay on my back on the ground and stared up at him.

"Hey, Bozo, you better watch where you're walking. You almost stepped into a big hole," Sammy said with a big laugh.

"A big hole in the middle of a green plastic field. It sounds like a miniature golf course to me. But that's silly. Everything on a miniature golf course is miniature," I said.

"Unless it is a giant miniature golf course," Sara interrupted.

I pulled myself up from the artificial grass and responded to Sara. "Why would you say that?"

"I didn't say that," she said. "The sign over there said it. I can't believe that we didn't see it before. It could have run us over, we were so close to it."

"The sign may not run us over, but there is a good chance that the big orange ball rolling toward us might," Brent said quickly.

"Golf course!" Sammy yelled.

"Big ball!" Sara screamed.

"Jump in the hole everyone," I commanded.

The other three went in before me. Once inside, we found ourselves sliding through a bent tube that led to a lower platform where there was a second hole.

We had to get to the bottom of the tube before the ball followed us. But that wasn't what happened.

Only seconds after I jumped into the hole, the ball fell in. Just our luck. The giant got a hole in one. We all slid down the tube with the ball behind us. It gained inches at a time. If it hit us, we would be crushed inside the tube.

I wondered how giants could exist and why they would play miniature golf.

Up ahead the tube split into two. To avoid getting crushed, we needed to go down one and the ball needed to go down another.

I yelled to the others, "Go down the left tube!"

Sara shifted her body and angled down the left side. Sammy and Brent followed. The ball was only a foot from my head. I had to take a gamble and go to the left. If the ball came after me that would be the end of the game. I slid feet first into the left tube and pushed off the side to give myself more speed so my head would clear the split before the ball got there.

The golf ball nailed the divider and bounced to the side. I prayed that it would go down the right side. I prayed hard. If ever I needed the Lord to answer my prayers, this was the time.

I looked back over my head. Was it going to follow me? I closed my eyes and kept sliding downward.

After a few seconds, I opened my eyes again and looked back. The ball was gone. It had gone down the right tube. In another moment I popped out the bottom and fell onto the artificial grass.

"How did you know that we needed to take the left one?" Brent asked me excitedly.

"I'll tell you as soon as we are off of this green," I answered. "As long as we are here, the ball can get us any time. I don't feel like repeating that last experience. Jump the wall."

We scrambled over the side and landed on another green.

"It looks like this is taking another bad turn," Sara whispered.

I nodded in agreement, then said, "Sara, if we get out of this one, then I'm heading straight for the front gate and back to my uncle's pool. I've decided that I don't need any more excitement in my life."

"Actually, things are looking up," Sammy assured us.

"How?" asked Sara.

"There's a number seventeen painted on this wall. That means we only have to get through two more holes," he informed us.

"Great, but I still want to know how Kyle knew that we should take the left tube," Brent insisted.

"It was easy. My dad and I play miniature golf all the time. Any time there is a split tube, the builders put in a slight bump to send the ball down the side farthest from the hole.

"I could see that the hole was near the opening on the left side. I assumed the ball would bounce down the right side."

"It saved us, Kyle. Thanks," Sammy added.

"Does anyone know where we should go now?" Brent quizzed.

"To get to the next hole we have to go through there."

Sara pointed to several large objects that were swinging back and forth. In their enlarged size, I couldn't tell what they were. I guessed the swinging objects were golf clubs.

"What do we have to do, Kyle?" Sara said, placing her hand on my shoulder.

"Avoid the next ball," Sammy called to us as he bolted from our spot toward the center of the fairway.

We turned our heads and saw another huge golf ball rolling toward us.

We leaped in step behind Sammy, running toward the clubs. We had little choice if we wanted to avoid the ball rolling toward us.

But the clubs were swinging back and forth in such a motion that we had to time it perfectly. And we didn't even have time to think, let alone plan our run.

Sara reached the clubs first. She was the most athletic one of us. She dodged and weaved. The first club missed her by only an inch. She let out a muffled scream.

She knew it was too close, but she couldn't turn back now.

The second one nipped her back heel. For a second she lost her balance. The delay worked in her favor. The third one went by easily. But I noticed that the fourth one moved at a faster rate of speed.

"Dive for it, Sara!" Sammy yelled. He must have noticed the speed increase as well.

Without hesitating, Sara did as she was told and

leaped forward like she was sliding into second base. It was a perfect base-stealing move.

Sammy faced the run next. I prayed that he'd be as attentive to his own run as he had been to Sara's. He ran past the first and stopped dead in his tracks as he waited for the second to pass him.

It worked.

Brent watched Sammy to plan his moves and made it through safely.

I was glad that they made it, but I had forgotten to watch out for my own run. The first club narrowly missed me. The second one tossed me into the air. I was flying.

The air rushed through my hair and I felt gravity pulling at the skin of my face.

I looked down and saw the other three watching me with their mouths open. I felt more like a bird than a boy.

The club threw me up and over the wall. I started my fall back to earth and then realized that the artificial grass on the other side of the wall was very near. That saved me from broken bones and maybe even worse when I hit the grass. I had not fallen far enough to pick up much momentum. "Kyle, are you all right?" Brent yelled up to me.

"I'm fine. You have got to get up here before the ball makes it through the clubs," I called down.

There was only one way and we all knew it. They

110

would have to let the clubs throw them over the wall. The giant's ball was already slicing through the barriers and would soon be rolling where they were standing.

The giant's ball bounced and hit the back wall. The ball rolled within a few feet of my friends.

"You've got to hitch a ride on one of the clubs and get up here before the next bounce nails you," I bellowed down to them.

My friends ran toward the clubs. The ball rolled even closer to them. The next time would get them for sure.

Sara leaped first. It was the perfect jump. She grabbed on with her hands and swung off the club as it reached the high point. She dropped down next to me.

Brent was caught by the club and flew much like I did to the top of the wall. He fell with more impact, and I heard his breath rush out of him. The only one left was Sammy.

He followed Sara's lead and grabbed on. His body flew off the club with great momentum, and the sound of him hitting the ground was loud.

He didn't move at first. He opened his eyes slowly. "I don't feel so good. Can we just go home now?" Sammy asked in a pained whisper.

"More than gladly, but first we have to get out of here," Sara said.

"What do we do now?" Brent asked.

I stood up and pointed to the next green. "If I am right, that should be the eighteenth hole and we are out of here.

I ran toward the hole and skidded to a stop. I had seen one of these before at Cascade Park Miniature Golf. It was the most difficult hole ever. The ball had to roll into a special cup at the exact time that a powerful blast of air shot out of the cup. The ball would fly into the air and fall into the hole.

I explained to the others what we had to do. Everyone understood except Sammy.

"So we get in the hole, then what?"

"The last hole is actually a tube that leads somewhere," I explained.

"Leads where?" Sammy asked.

"Out. I hope," I told him. "I hope—and pray."

We only had two choices. We could stay and risk getting crushed by a giant golf ball or we could risk getting into the last hole. The second choice provided the best chance to escape.

"Brent, you go first. Sammy, you go second, and Sara, since you're the fastest, you'll need to go third.

There won't be any time for mistakes. Since I know the hole the best, I'll go last. Keep moving once you're on the green in case a ball heads our way," I instructed them.

We had all just jumped to the eighteenth green when Sammy yelled, "Look out!"

Another ball was rolling toward us as Brent headed for the cup and the blast of air. He leaped in the cup and the air blasted him upward. He dropped into the hole and was out of sight.

Sammy was in the cup before Brent reached the hole. Sammy flew upward, but he twisted wrong and came back down into the cup. I turned around and saw the ball rolling closer to Sara and me.

"I don't think we're going to make it before the ball arrives. Watch yourself as you run for the cup. Keep looking back because that ball is going to head for the hole as well."

I turned to look at Sammy. He was just dropping into the hole. That was two of us safe. Sara raced across the green. The ball was right behind her. She dived for the cup, and the blast of air shot her straight upward.

The ball was so close to her that the rushing air pushed it backward. I was glad she beat the golf ball, but it was heading back toward me.

Sara dropped inside the hole. I was the only one left. The ball was rolling my way.

As the orange ball rolled back toward me I felt a rumble and saw a white one moving up behind me. I was about to be sandwiched between two golf balls.

I looked in front of me and then behind me. The two were about equal distance from me. I could not run fast enough to get away from the rolling menaces.

As the balls approached, I dived from between them. They hit each other and flew off in different directions. I lay on the artificial turf, watching them.

The orange one bounced off the wall and came directly toward me. I rolled out of its way.

This was a good short-term solution, but I needed a long-term one that would send me sliding down the eighteenth hole. I jumped to my feet and started jamming my tennis shoes into the turf. I picked up speed, but so did the white ball. I hit the cup and was propelled into the air. I saw the hole that I needed to drop into below me. I twisted my body and down I went into the escape route.

I dropped out of the chute into the middle of my friends. I looked up to see who pulled me up. Sammy and Brent smiled back at me.

"We did it. We got out of there," I told them with relief showing across my face. "Where are we now?"

Sammy pointed to a door. "Sara went over to that door to see what was on the other side. She'll be back in a minute. Just take a break and rest."

"I don't think we should do that. A golf ball will be heading out of that hole in a second," I said.

We scrambled to our feet and ran for the door. Sara was waiting for us.

Sara smiled when she saw us. "I think this is all over," she yelled. "On the other side of this door is the nicest sight I've seen all day."

We opened the door and before us was a sign that said, Transylvania Tram to Dr. Shivers' Carnival of Terror. We were finally out of the Tunnel of the Weird and on our way home, or at least to the place that led to home.

"All aboard," said a voice from the speaker system above our heads. We slipped through the doors into a brand-new tram car. It looked more like a small subway car, but that didn't make any difference to us.

Our feet hurt and we were tired.

Brent stared at the walls around us. "Doesn't it seem strange that there isn't another person on this tram?" he asked.

"No, what's strange to me is that in one night Dr. Shivers could have set up a carnival and a tram system. I'm beginning to think that there is more to this place than we can see," I told them.

The tram slowed down and came to a stop. I looked out the window. It wasn't our stop. The sign read Wereville. I thought that was a strange name for a town. "We have stopped at Wereville."

"What an odd name for a town. I wonder what it

means. I wonder how you're supposed to pronounce it," Sammy added, "*where-* or *were-* or *we're*-ville?"

"Quiet. The door is opening and someone's getting on," Brent whispered to us.

A boy about our age slid through the open door. He smiled at us and said hello. We all returned his greeting. He sat down at the other end of the tram car.

When he did, the Wereville sign shook. The *I* shifted and then spun around.

"There's our next clue," Sara said. "*It's only a m-o-i.*"

"It's only a moist cookie," Sammy guessed.

"That's silly. Why would the mysterious clues lead us to *It's only a moist cookie?*" Brent scoffed.

"They don't. There was another letter after the *O*," I told them. "When we were at the game booth with the mask, the man there gave me the victory sign. You know, *V.*"

"Then it's *M-O-V-I,*" Sara said thoughtfully.

Sammy looked at the sign distractedly and asked, "What do they say in Wereville? Do they say *where* in *Wereville*? Or do they say *we're* in Wereville?"

"Or is it the werewolf of Wereville?" Sara joked, giving up on the mystery clues for a moment.

"The werewolf of Wereville," I said slowly. Then I said it again, "The werewolf of Wereville. That has a nice ring to it."

"Next you will be saying that the guy sitting down there is a werewolf," Brent said, chuckling.

We all laughed at Brent's joke and sat back in our seats. We were exhausted and needed to rest. The only sound was that of the tram moving over the tracks. The clickety-clack soothed me and I closed my eyes.

I was just about asleep when the tram slowed down again. I groggily asked, "Where are we?"

Brent put his face to the glass and looked outside. He turned around and told us that this stop was called Full Moon Junction.

"Werewolf of Wereville traveling through Full Moon Junction. Can this get any stranger?" I asked.

As I joked, the boy at the other end of the tram started to twitch and jerk. He held a hand up in the air. It was covered with hair. Then he leaped to his feet and growled. The boy twisted in the other direction and ran into the next car.

"What was that?" Sammy asked.

"It was really weird," Brent added.

"It was also a werewolf. He got on at Wereville, and then when we passed through Full Moon Junction the boy started to transform into a werewolf. Any minute now, he will walk through that door with only one thing on his mind," I explained.

"What?" Sara asked.

"Dinner. We are going to be his dinner," I expressed with unnatural calmness.

"Do you have any suggestions?" Sammy quizzed.

The doors to the other tram car opened and the werewolf leaped through them.

"I have one suggestion—run!" I yelled loudly.

We all ran from our tram car to the next one. The werewolf didn't waste any time. He smashed into the door and then through it.

We only had a few seconds to open the next door and leap through it. The werewolf jumped from seat to seat. He was tearing them up with his claws.

Sammy used his belt to tie the door handle to one of the metal bars people use to steady themselves. The belt held for a few minutes.

The werewolf got madder and madder as he hit and pulled at the door.

"How many more tram cars do we have till we reach the end?" I asked.

Sammy pulled open the door and looked inside. When he turned around, his eyes were filled with real fright. "The next car is the last one, and it's filled with all kinds of boxes and junk. There's no place to run after that one."

"Great!" Sara said.

"What do you mean great? We could be dinner for a werewolf and you say that's great?"

Sammy was getting more animated as he spoke. His arms were flying in the air and his eyes were bugging out.

"I don't want to get eaten. I just want out of here."

The belt holding out the werewolf was stretching. The leather showed signs of splitting. I didn't think that we had more than another minute to move to the next car.

"Let's get into that other car. Once we're there we can block the door with boxes," I called to my friends.

We yanked open the last door just as the werewolf ripped the leather belt. The werewolf's yellow eyes glared at us as he let out a tremendous howl.

Sammy, Sara, and I passed into the last tram car. After Brent joined us, Sara slammed the door shut behind him, picked up a broom that lay on the floor and jammed it into the door to hold it shut. The werewolf smashed his face against the glass of the door. His hot breath steamed the window.

We backed against the junk in the last car and started looking and scrambling through the boxes.

"I found something that might work," Brent yelled out as he pulled a chain from under a stack of rags.

He and Sammy ran to the door and wrapped the chain through the handle and around the bottom of a spare seat stored in the car.

"What do we lock it with, Brent?" Sammy asked.

"I don't know. What can we lock it with, Kyle?"

I found a small rope. I looked at it and then looked back at the chain. It could work, but then the chain could still break. We didn't have a lot of choices. I tossed it to Brent. "Try this. It won't hold for long, but it will keep him out while we try to figure out something else."

Brent and Sammy tied the chain together with the rope and wrapped it as tightly as they could.

The werewolf continued to smash his body against the door. His howls were getting louder.

I glanced around at my friends. Fear strained their faces as they wildly tore through the boxes of junk, looking for something to use for protection. We were reacting out of panic. I needed to say something to calm everyone down. In a flash I knew everything would be all right.

"Hey, we've been in some pretty tight spots in Dr. Shivers' carnival, but the Lord got us out of each one, right? What are we so worried about? The werewolf could change back any minute or turn around and run off the tram."

Sara stared at me. The tension was getting to us all. I had to do something to get rid of this werewolf and save my friends. I climbed down off the stack of boxes and spotted a shovel. I picked it up and walked toward the door.

Sammy stepped between the door and me. "What are you doing?" he asked.

"I'm going to get us out of this. When I open the door and smash the werewolf with the shovel, you guys jump out the back door. Run as fast as you can, and I'll hold him off as long as I can."

My voice quivered with fear as I spoke.

One of us had to stop him, and it was going to be me. I pushed Sammy out of the way and took a few more steps toward the door. Suddenly the tram lurched forward, then backward. I didn't have to walk the last few steps to the door. The tram tossed me toward the door, and I hit it with a heavy thud.

The werewolf was just inches away.

The werewolf was pressed against the other side of the window. His fierce eyes glowered at me.

The tram had come to a complete stop. The werewolf backed up. I thought he was getting ready to run right through the door.

I bent down and picked up my shovel. He was not going to get through me.

When I stood up again, he was gone. I thought he might be hiding. I waited. The werewolf could attack again, and I wanted to be ready for him.

"Look!" Brent screamed with excitement. "The werewolf got off at this stop. We are safe."

"Where are we?" Sara asked.

Sammy looked at the nearest sign. "This is the stop for Monster Middle School. Why would he be out of school at this time of the day?"

"He went out for lunch. We were going to be his fast food. 'I'll take four kids, please, and hold the mustard,'" Sammy blurted out.

I started laughing. Then Sara picked it up, then Brent. We kept laughing until the tram began moving again. As we pulled away from the Monster Middle School, a voice came over the speaker above us.

"Last stop coming up, Dr. Shivers' Carnival of Terror. We hope you enjoyed your ride. Please ride the Transylvania Tram again soon."

"Finally, we're back at the carnival. I never thought that I'd be glad to be back at the Carnival of Terror," Sara said. We all agreed as we sat motionless, waiting to see the carnival up ahead. The tram came to a slow and easy stop. The door opened and we entered an enclosed area. Up ahead was a large Exit sign, but only the *E* was lit up. It was in that second that Sara and I turned to each other and said in unison, *"It's only a movie!"*

We stumbled into the sunlight and out onto the midway. There we saw the clown and several others walking toward us.

Something was different about the clown. He had taken off his makeup. I recognized him. I couldn't believe who it was.

It was Uncle Rex. Behind him were several men and women with clipboards and communication headsets. We ran up to him.

"Uncle Rex, you've got to have this place closed down. It's too frightening. Kids will be scared to death here. Dr. Shivers has monsters that tried to eat us and rides that tried to knock us off. He even has giants that play miniature golf."

The words tumbled out of my mouth.

Finally, it hit me—Uncle Rex was wearing the clown suit. I was puzzled.

"Uncle Rex, why are you dressed like a clown?"

Then I heard a gruesome laugh come from behind me. I spun around and saw Dr. Shivers. He looked different as well. Brent gasped.

Uncle Rex looked at me. "Great! You kids were great."

We must have given him the most puzzled looks he ever saw. He started to laugh. "Kids, I wanted you all to come to this carnival."

"Why? Did my dad do something to you when you were a kid that you needed to get revenge for?" I asked.

"No, this is the set for a made-for-TV movie. If it goes well, it will be a new series called, of course, 'Dr. Shivers' Carnival of Terror.' I wanted to test the rides on kids who didn't know anything about them. We wanted four kids from the Midwest. So I called your dad and told him what I had planned. You four were fantastic."

Sara's face broke into a big smile. "Then everything we saw was made by illusions and special effects?"

"Exactly," Uncle Rex answered.

"Then I never ate any worms?" Brent said with relief.

"Nope, it was real cotton candy with a hologram inside it. Pretty neat, huh?" my uncle responded. "Now, I want you to meet Dr. Shivers. I'm sure you recognize him. This is Johnny Tate."

Brent looked at him with a smug smile. "I knew you looked familiar," he said, giving the famous teen television star an I-knew-it-all-along look.

"Then we were right about the clues spelling out *It's only a movie*," I said.

"Yep. I've been concerned by all the horror books middle school kids are reading. Even worse is that some of them believe that stuff. I want kids to have fun, but they need to separate what's of God and what's of the imagination," Uncle Rex explained.

"How did you get us to follow the correct order for the letters?" Brent wondered out loud.

Uncle Rex smiled and put his arm around Sammy. "Last night I filled Sammy in on the whole plan. He guided you to the clues.

"And we filmed everything you kids did. Mostly we wanted to see how you'd react. We'll use those scenes for the opening credits of the TV movie. And better yet, you'll all get paid for it," my uncle rattled on.

Sammy jumped in front of me. "Do you mean we'll be on TV? I'll be a star?"

"Kind of, Sammy. In fact, you gave us some of our best footage. After we take it back to the studio and make the edits and cuts, I'll bring it home for you all to see.

"Now, I need to get my crew together to close things down. Why don't you kids head back to the house and we'll have dinner together," Uncle Rex said.

"Will Johnny Tate be coming?" Sara asked.

"I wouldn't have it any other way," Uncle Rex responded.

All the danger, all the excitement, had only been gimmicks and tricks. I felt a little sheepish, but mostly I felt relieved. *Thank You, Lord*, I prayed. *I should've known You were in charge all along.*

We had started back to the gate when my uncle called, "Hey, Sammy, catch."

Through the air came the barking hot dog. Sammy caught it and we all laughed. He got his souvenir of Dr. Shivers' Carnival of Terror after all.

As we walked back to the house, Sammy nudged me and said, "There's nothing like this back in our little town."